JOHN STEINBECK

CANNERY ROW

PENGUIN BOOKS

PENGUIN BOOKS
Published by the Penguin Group
Penguin Books USA Inc.,
375 Hudson Street, New York, New York 10014, U.S.A.
Penguin Books Ltd, 27 Wrights Lane, London W8 5TZ, England
Penguin Books Australia Ltd, Ringwood, Victoria, Australia
Penguin Books Canada Ltd, 10 Alcorn Avenue,
Toronto, Ontario, Canada M4V 3B2
Penguin Books (N.Z.) Ltd, 182–190 Wairau Road,
Auckland 10, New Zealand

Penguin Books Ltd, Registered Offices:
Harmondsworth, Middlesex, England

First published in the United States of America by
The Viking Press Inc., 1945
First published in a volume with
Of Mice and Men in Penguin Books 1978
This edition published 1992

19   20   18

ISBN 0 14 01.7738 8

Printed in the United States of America
Set in Bodoni Book

For
ED RICKETTS
who knows why or should

CANNERY ROW

CANNERY ROW

Cannery Row in Monterey in California is a poem, a stink, a grating noise, a quality of light, a tone, a habit, a nostalgia, a dream. Cannery Row is the gathered and scattered, tin and iron and rust and splintered wood, chipped pavement and weedy lots and junk heaps, sardine canneries of corrugated iron, honky tonks, restaurants and whore houses, and little crowded groceries, and laboratories and flophouses. Its inhabitants are, as the man once said, "whores, pimps, gamblers, and sons of bitches," by which he meant Everybody. Had the man looked through another peephole he might have said, "Saints and angels and martyrs and holy men," and he would have meant the same thing.

In the morning when the sardine fleet has made a catch, the purse-seiners waddle heavily into the bay blowing their whistles. The deep-laden boats pull in against the coast where the canneries dip their tails into the bay. The figure is advisedly chosen, for if the canneries dipped their mouths into the bay the canned sardines which emerge from the other end would be metaphorically, at least, even more horrifying. Then cannery whistles scream and all over the town men and women scramble into their clothes and come running down to the Row to go to work. Then shining cars bring the upper classes down: superintendents, accountants, owners who disappear into offices. Then from the town pour Wops and Chinamen and Polaks, men and women in trousers and rubber coats and oilcloth aprons. They come running to clean and cut and pack and cook and can the fish. The whole street rumbles and groans and screams and rattles while the silver rivers of fish pour in out of the boats and the boats rise higher and higher in the water until they are empty. The canneries rumble and rattle and squeak until the last fish is cleaned and cut and cooked and canned and then the whistles scream again and the dripping, smelly, tired Wops and Chinamen and Polaks, men and women, straggle out and droop their ways up the hill into the town and Cannery Row becomes itself again—quiet and magical. Its normal life returns. The bums who retired in disgust under the black cypress tree come out to sit on the rusty pipes in the vacant lot. The girls from Dora's emerge for a bit of sun if there is any. Doc strolls from the Western Biological Laboratory and crosses the street to Lee Chong's grocery for two quarts of beer. Henri the painter noses like an Airedale through the junk in the grass-grown lot for some part or piece of wood or metal he needs for the boat he is building. Then the darkness edges in and the street light comes on in front of Dora's—the lamp which makes perpetual moonlight in Cannery Row. Callers arrive at Western Biological to see Doc, and he crosses the street to Lee Chong's for five quarts of beer.

How can the poem and the stink and the grating noise—the quality of light, the tone, the habit and the dream—be set down alive? When you collect marine animals there are certain flat worms so delicate that they are almost impossible to capture whole, for they break and tatter under the touch. You must let them ooze and crawl of their own will onto a knife blade and then lift them gently into your bottle of sea water. And perhaps that might be the way to write this book—to open the page and to let the stories crawl in by themselves.

1

Lee Chong's grocery, while not a model of neatness, was a miracle of supply. It was small and crowded but within its single room a man could find everything he needed or wanted to live and to be happy—clothes, food, both fresh and canned, liquor, tobacco, fishing equipment, machinery, boats, cordage, caps, pork chops. You could buy at Lee Chong's a pair of slippers, a silk kimono, a quarter pint of whiskey and a cigar. You could work out combinations to fit almost any mood. The one commodity Lee Chong did not keep could be had across the lot at Dora's.

The grocery opened at dawn and did not close until the last wandering vagrant dime had been spent or retired for the night. Not that Lee Chong was avaricious. He wasn't, but if one wanted to spend money, he was available. Lee's position in the community surprised him as much as he could be surprised. Over the course of the years everyone in Cannery Row owed him money. He never pressed his clients, but when the bill became too large, Lee cut off credit. Rather than walk into the town up the hill, the client usually paid or tried to.

Lee was round-faced and courteous. He spoke a stately English without ever using the letter R. When the tong wars were going on in California, it happened now and then that Lee found a price on his head. Then he would go secretly to San Francisco and enter a hospital until the trouble blew over. What he did with his money, no one ever knew. Perhaps he didn't get it. Maybe his wealth was entirely in unpaid bills. But he lived well and he had the respect of all his neighbors. He trusted his clients until further trust became ridiculous. Sometimes he made business errors, but even these he turned to advantage in good will if in no other way. It was that way with the Palace Flophouse and Grill. Anyone but Lee Chong would have considered the transaction a total loss.

Lee Chong's station in the grocery was behind the cigar counter. The cash register was then on his left and the abacus on his right. Inside the glass case were the brown cigars, the cigarettes, the Bull Durham, the Duke's mixture, the Five Brothers, while behind him in racks on the wall were the pints, half pints and quarters of Old Green River, Old Town House, Old Colonel, and the favorite—Old Tennessee, a blended whiskey guaranteed four months old, very cheap and known in the neighborhood as Old Tennis Shoes. Lee Chong did not stand between the whiskey and the customer without reason. Some very practical minds had on occasion tried to divert his attention to another part of the store. Cousins, nephews, sons and daughters-in-law waited on the rest of the store, but Lee never left the cigar counter. The top of the glass was his desk. His fat delicate hands rested on the glass, the fingers moving like small restless sausages. A broad golden wedding ring on the middle finger of his left hand was his only jewelry and with it he silently tapped on the rubber change mat from which the little rubber tits had long been worn. Lee's mouth was full and benevolent and the flash of gold when he smiled was rich and warm. He wore half-glasses and since he looked at everything through them, he had to tilt his head back to see in the distance. Interest and discounts, addition, subtraction he worked out on the abacus with his little restless sausage fingers, and his brown friendly eyes roved over the grocery and his teeth flashed at the customers.

On an evening when he stood in his place on a pad of newspaper to keep his feet warm, he contemplated with humor and sadness a business deal that had been consummated that afternoon and reconsummated later that same afternoon. When you leave the grocery, if you walk catty-cornered across the grass-grown lot, threading your way among the great rusty pipes thrown out of the canneries, you will see a path worn in the weeds. Follow it past the cypress tree, across the railroad track, up a chicken walk with cleats, and you will come to a long low building which for a long time was used as a storage place for fish meal. It was just a great big roofed room and it belonged to a worried gentleman named Horace Abbeville. Horace had two wives and six children and over a period of years he had managed through pleading and persuasion to build a grocery debt second to none in Monterey. That afternoon he had come into the grocery and his sensitive tired face had flinched at the shadow of sternness that crossed Lee's face. Lee's fat finger tapped the rubber mat. Horace laid his hands palm up on the cigar counter. "I guess I owe you plenty dough," he said simply.

Lee's teeth flashed up in appreciation of an approach so different from any he had ever heard. He nodded gravely, but he waited for the trick to develop.

Horace wet his lips with his tongue, a good job from corner to corner. "I hate to have my kids with that hanging over them," he said. "Why, I bet you wouldn't let them have a pack of spearmint now."

Lee Chong's face agreed with this conclusion. "Plenty dough," he said.

Horace continued, "You know that place of mine across the track up there where the fish meal is."

Lee Chong nodded. It was his fish meal.

Horace said earnestly, "If I was to give you that place—would it clear me up with you?"

Lee Chong tilted his head back and stared at Horace through his half-glasses while his mind flicked among accounts and his right hand moved restlessly to the abacus. He considered the construction which was flimsy and the lot which might be valuable if a cannery ever wanted to expand. "Shu," said Lee Chong.

"Well, get out the accounts and I'll make you a bill of sale on that place." Horace seemed in a hurry.

"No need papers," said Lee. "I make paid-in-full paper."

They finished the deal with dignity and Lee Chong threw in a quarter pint of Old Tennis Shoes. And then Horace Abbeville walking very straight went across the lot and past the cypress tree and across the track and up the chicken walk and into the building that had been his, and he shot himself on a heap of fish meal. And although it has nothing to do with this story, no Abbeville child, no matter who its mother was, knew the lack of a stick of spearmint ever afterward.

But to get back to the evening. Horace was on the trestles with the embalming needles in him, and his two wives were sitting on the steps of his house with their arms about each other (they were good friends until after the funeral, and then they divided up the children and never spoke to each other again). Lee Chong stood in back of the cigar counter and his nice brown eyes were turned inward on a calm and eternal Chinese sorrow. He knew he could not have helped it, but he wished he might have known and perhaps tried to help. It was deeply a part of Lee's kindness and understanding that man's right to kill himself is inviolable, but sometimes a friend can make it unnecessary. Lee had already underwritten the funeral and sent a wash basket of groceries to the stricken families.

Now Lee Chong owned the Abbeville building—a good roof, a good floor, two windows and a door. True it was piled high with fish meal and the smell of it was delicate and penetrating. Lee Chong considered it as a storehouse for groceries, as a kind of warehouse, but he gave that up on second thought. It was too far away and anyone can go in through a window. He was tapping the rubber mat with his gold ring and considering the problem when the door opened and Mack came in. Mack was the elder, leader, mentor, and to a small extent the exploiter of a little group of men who had in common no families, no money, and no ambitions beyond food, drink, and contentment. But whereas most

men in their search for contentment destroy themselves and fall wearily short of their targets, Mack and
his friends approached contentment casually, quietly,
and absorbed it gently. Mack and Hazel, a young man
of great strength, Eddie who filled in as a bartender at
La Ida, Hughie and Jones who occasionally collected
frogs and cats for Western Biological, were currently
living in those large rusty pipes in the lot next to Lee
Chong's. That is, they lived in the pipes when it was
damp but in fine weather they lived in the shadow of
the black cypress tree at the top of the lot. The limbs
folded down and made a canopy under which a man
could lie and look out at the flow and vitality of Cannery Row.

Lee Chong stiffened ever so slightly when Mack
came in and his eyes glanced quickly about the store
to make sure that Eddie or Hazel or Hughie or Jones
had not come in too and drifted away among the
groceries.

Mack laid out his cards with a winning honesty.
"Lee," he said, "I and Eddie and the rest heard you
own the Abbeville place."

Lee Chong nodded and waited.

"I and my friends thought we'd ast you if we could
move in there. We'll keep up the property," he added
quickly. "Wouldn't let anybody break in or hurt anything. Kids might knock out the windows, you know—"
Mack suggested. "Place might burn down if somebody
don't keep an eye on it."

Lee tilted his head back and looked into Mack's
eyes through the half-glasses and Lee's tapping finger
slowed its tempo as he thought deeply. In Mack's eyes

there was good will and good fellowship and a desire to make everyone happy. Why then did Lee Chong feel slightly surrounded? Why did his mind pick its way as delicately as a cat through cactus? It had been sweetly done, almost in a spirit of philanthropy. Lee's mind leaped ahead at the possibilities—no, they were probabilities, and his finger tapping slowed still further. He saw himself refusing Mack's request and he saw the broken glass from the windows. Then Mack would offer a second time to watch over and preserve Lee's property—and at the second refusal, Lee could smell the smoke, could see the little flames creeping up the walls. Mack and his friends would try to help to put it out. Lee's finger came to a gentle rest on the change mat. He was beaten. He knew that. There was left to him only the possibility of saving face and Mack was likely to be very generous about that. Lee said, "You like pay lent my place? You like live there same hotel?"

Mack smiled broadly and he was generous. "Say—" he cried. "That's an idear. Sure. How much?"

Lee considered. He knew it didn't matter what he charged. He wasn't going to get it anyway. He might just as well make it a really sturdy face-saving sum. "Fi' dolla' week," said Lee.

Mack played it through to the end. "I'll have to talk to the boys about it," he said dubiously. "Couldn't you make that four dollars a week?"

"Fi' dolla'," said Lee firmly.

"Well, I'll see what the boys say," said Mack.

And that was the way it was. Everyone was happy about it. And if it be thought that Lee Chong suffered a total loss, at least his mind did not work that way. The windows were not broken. Fire did not break out, and while no rent was ever paid, if the tenants ever had any money, and quite often they did have, it never occurred to them to spend it any place except at Lee Chong's grocery. What he had was a little group of active and potential customers under wraps. But it went further than that. If a drunk caused trouble in the grocery, if the kids swarmed down from New Monterey intent on plunder, Lee Chong had only to call and his tenants rushed to his aid. One further bond it established—you cannot steal from your benefactor. The saving to Lee Chong in cans of beans and tomatoes and milk and watermelons more than paid the rent. And if there was a sudden and increased leakage among the groceries in New Monterey that was none of Lee Chong's affair.

The boys moved in and the fish meal moved out. No one knows who named the house that has been known ever after as the Palace Flophouse and Grill. In the pipes and under the cypress tree there had been no room for furniture and the little niceties which are not only the diagnoses but the boundaries of our civilization. Once in the Palace Flophouse, the boys set about furnishing it. A chair appeared and a cot and another chair. A hardware store supplied a can of red paint not reluctantly because it never knew about it, and as a new table or footstool appeared it was painted, which not only made it very pretty but also disguised it to a certain extent in case a former owner looked in. And the Palace Flophouse and Grill began to function. The boys could sit in front of their door and look down

across the track and across the lot and across the
street right into the front windows of Western Biological. They could hear the music from the laboratory at
night. And their eyes followed Doc across the street
when he went to Lee Chong's for beer. And Mack said,
"That Doc is a fine fellow. We ought to do something
for him."

2

The word is a symbol and a delight which sucks up men and scenes, trees, plants, factories, and Pekinese. Then the Thing becomes the Word and back to Thing again, but warped and woven into a fantastic pattern. The Word sucks up Cannery Row, digests it and spews it out, and the Row has taken the shimmer of the green world and the sky-reflecting seas. Lee Chong is more than a Chinese grocer. He must be. Perhaps he is evil balanced and held suspended by good—an Asiatic planet held to its orbit by the pull of Lao Tze and held away from Lao Tze by the centrifugality of abacus and cash register—Lee Chong suspended, spinning, whirling among groceries and ghosts. A hard man with a can of beans—a soft man with the bones of his grandfather. For Lee Chong dug into the grave on China Point and found the yellow bones, the skull with gray ropy hair still sticking to it. And Lee carefully packed the bones, femurs, and tibias really straight, skull in the middle, with pelvis and clavicle surrounding it and ribs curving on either side. Then Lee Chong sent his boxed and brittle grandfather over the western sea to lie at last in ground made holy by his ancestors.

Mack and the boys, too, spinning in their orbits. They are the Virtues, the Graces, the Beauties of the hurried mangled craziness of Monterey and the cosmic Monterey where men in fear and hunger destroy their stomachs in the fight to secure certain food, where men hungering for love destroy everything lovable about them. Mack and the boys are the Beauties, the Virtues, the Graces. In the world ruled by tigers with ulcers, rutted by strictured bulls, scavenged by blind jackals, Mack and the boys dine delicately with the tigers, fondle the frantic heifers, and wrap up the crumbs to feed the sea gulls of Cannery Row. What can it profit a man to gain the whole world and to come to his property with a gastric ulcer, a blown prostate, and bifocals? Mack and the boys avoid the trap, walk around the poison, step over the noose while a generation of trapped, poisoned, and trussed-up men scream at them and call them no-goods, come-to-bad-ends, blots-on-the-town, thieves, rascals, bums. Our Father who art in nature, who has given the gift of survival to the coyote, the common brown rat, the English sparrow, the house fly and the moth, must have a great and overwhelming love for no-goods and blots-on-the-town and bums, and Mack and the boys. Virtues and graces and laziness and zest. Our Father who art in nature.

3

Lee Chong's is to the right of the vacant lot (although why it is called vacant when it is piled high with old boilers, with rusting pipes, with great square timbers, and stacks of five-gallon cans, no one can say). Up in back of the vacant lot is the railroad track and the Palace Flophouse. But on the left-hand boundary of the lot is the stern and stately whore house of Dora Flood; a decent, clean, honest, old-fashioned sporting house where a man can take a glass of beer among friends. This is no fly-by-night cheap clip-joint but a sturdy, virtuous club, built, maintained, and disciplined by Dora who, madam and girl for fifty years, has through the exercise of special gifts of tact and honesty, charity and a certain realism, made herself respected by the intelligent, the learned, and the kind. And by the same token she is hated by the twisted and lascivious sisterhood of married spinsters whose husbands respect the home but don't like it very much.

Dora is a great woman, a great big woman with flaming orange hair and a taste for Nile green evening dresses. She keeps an honest, one price house, sells no hard liquor, and permits no loud or vulgar talk in her house. Of her girls some are fairly inactive due to age and infirmities, but Dora never puts them aside although, as she says, some of them don't turn three tricks a month but they go right on eating three meals a day. In a moment of local love Dora named her place the Bear Flag Restaurant and the stories are many of people who have gone in for a sandwich. There are normally twelve girls in the house, counting the old ones, a Greek cook, and a man who is known as a watchman but who undertakes all manner of delicate and dangerous tasks. He stops fights, ejects drunks, soothes hysteria, cures headaches, and tends bar. He bandages cuts and bruises, passes the time of day with cops, and since a good half of the girls are Christian Scientists, reads aloud his share of *Science and Health* on a Sunday morning. His predecessor, being a less well-balanced man, came to an evil end as shall be reported, but Alfred has triumphed over his environment and has brought his environment up with him. He knows what men should be there and what men shouldn't be there. He knows more about the home life of Monterey citizens than anyone in town.

As for Dora—she leads a ticklish existence. Being against the law, at least against its letter, she must be twice as law abiding as anyone else. There must be no drunks, no fighting, no vulgarity, or they close Dora up. Also being illegal Dora must be especially philanthropic. Everyone puts the bite on her. If the police give a dance for their pension fund and everyone else gives a dollar, Dora has to give fifty dollars. When the Chamber of Commerce improved its gardens, the merchants

each gave five dollars but Dora was asked for and gave a
hundred. With everything else it is the same, Red
Cross, Community Chest, Boy Scouts, Dora's unsung,
unpublicized, shameless dirty wages of sin lead the list
of donations. But during the depression she was hardest
hit. In addition to the usual charities, Dora saw the
hungry children of Cannery Row and the jobless fathers
and the worried women and Dora paid grocery bills
right and left for two years and very nearly went broke
in the process. Dora's girls are well trained and pleasant. They never speak to a man on the street although
he may have been in the night before.

Before Alfy the present watchman took over, there
was a tragedy in the Bear Flag Restaurant which saddened everyone. The previous watchman was named
William and he was a dark and lonesome-looking man.
In the daytime when his duties were few he would
grow tired of female company. Through the windows
he could see Mack and the boys sitting on the pipes in
the vacant lot, dangling their feet in the mallow weeds
and taking the sun while they discoursed slowly and
philosophically of matters of interest but of no impor-
tance. Now and then as he watched them he saw them
take out a pint of Old Tennis Shoes and wiping the
neck of the bottle on a sleeve, raise the pint one after
another. And William began to wish he could join that
good group. He walked out one day and sat on the
pipe. Conversation stopped and an uneasy and hostile
silence fell on the group. After a while William went
disconsolately back to the Bear Flag and through the
window he saw the conversation spring up again and it
saddened him. He had a dark and ugly face and a
mouth twisted with brooding.

The next day he went again and this time he took a pint of whiskey. Mack and the boys drank the whiskey, after all they weren't crazy, but all the talking they did was "Good luck," and "Lookin' at you."

After a while William went back to the Bear Flag and he watched them through the window and he heard Mack raise his voice saying, "But God damn it, I hate a pimp!" Now this was obviously untrue although William didn't know that. Mack and the boys just didn't like William.

Now William's heart broke. The bums would not receive him socially. They felt that he was too far beneath them. William had always been introspective and self-accusing. He put on his hat and walked out along the sea, clear out to the Lighthouse. And he stood in the pretty little cemetery where you can hear the waves drumming always. William thought dark and broody thoughts. No one loved him. No one cared about him. They might call him a watchman but he was a pimp—a dirty pimp, the lowest thing in the world. And then he thought how he had a right to live and be happy just like anyone else, by God he had. He walked back angrily but his anger went away when he came to the Bear Flag and climbed the steps. It was evening and the juke box was playing *Harvest Moon* and William remembered that the first hooker who ever gaffed for him used to like that song before she ran away and got married and disappeared. The song made him awfully sad. Dora was in the back parlor having a cup of tea when William came in. She said, "What's the matter, you sick?"

"No," said William. "But what's the percentage? I feel lousy. I think I'll bump myself off."

Dora had handled plenty of neurotics in her time. Kid 'em out of it was her motto. "Well, do it on your own time and don't mess up the rugs," she said.

A gray damp cloud folded over William's heart and he walked slowly out and down the hall and knocked on Eva Flanegan's door. She had red hair and went to confession every week. Eva was quite a spiritual girl with a big family of brothers and sisters but she was an unpredictable drunk. She was painting her nails and messing them pretty badly when William went in and he knew she was bagged and Dora wouldn't let a bagged girl work. Her fingers were nail polish to the first joint and she was angry. "What's eating you?" she said. William grew angry too. "I'm going to bump myself off," he said fiercely.

Eva screeched at him. "That's a dirty, lousy, stinking sin," she cried, and then, "Wouldn't it be like you to get the joint pinched just when I got almost enough kick to take a trip to East St. Louis. You're a no-good bastard." She was still screaming at him when William shut her door after him and went to the kitchen. He was very tired of women. The Greek would be restful after women.

The Greek, big apron, sleeves rolled up, was frying pork chops in two big skillets, turning them over with an ice pick. "Hello, Kits. How is going things?" The pork chops hissed and swished in the pan.

"I don't know, Lou," said William. "Sometimes I think the best thing to do would be—kluck!" He drew his finger across his throat.

The Greek laid the ice pick on the stove and rolled his sleeves higher. "I tell you what I hear, Kits," he said. "I hear like the fella talks about it don't never do it." William's hand went out for the ice pick and he held it easily in his hand. His eyes looked deeply into the Greek's dark eyes and he saw disbelief and amusement and then as he stared the Greek's eyes grew troubled and then worried. And William saw the change, saw first how the Greek knew he could do it and then the Greek knew he would do it. As soon as he saw that in the Greek's eyes William knew he had to do it. He was sad because now it seemed silly. His hand rose and the ice pick snapped into his heart. It was amazing how easily it went in. William was the watchman before Alfred came. Everyone liked Alfred. He could sit on the pipes with Mack and the boys any time. He could even visit up at the Palace Flophouse.

4

In the evening just at dusk, a curious thing happened on Cannery Row. It happened in the time between sunset and the lighting of the street light. There is a small quiet gray period then. Down the hill, past the Palace Flophouse, down the chicken walk and through the vacant lot came an old Chinaman. He wore an ancient flat straw hat, blue jeans, both coat and trousers, and heavy shoes of which one sole was loose so that it slapped the ground when he walked. In his hand he carried a covered wicker basket. His face was lean and brown and corded as jerky and his old eyes were brown, even the whites were brown and deep set so that they looked out of holes. He came by just at dusk and crossed the street and went through the opening between Western Biological and the Hediondo Cannery. Then he crossed the little beach and disappeared among the piles and steel posts which support the piers. No one saw him again until dawn.

But in the dawn, during that time when the street light has been turned off and the daylight has not

come, the old Chinaman crept out from among the
piles, crossed the beach and the street. His wicker
basket was heavy and wet and dripping now. His loose
sole flap-flapped on the street. He went up the hill to
the second street, went through a gate in a high board
fence and was not seen again until evening. People,
sleeping, heard his flapping shoe go by and they awakened for a moment. It had been happening for years
but no one ever got used to him. Some people thought
he was God and very old people thought he was Death
and children thought he was a very funny old Chinaman, as children always think anything old and
strange is funny. But the children did not taunt him or
shout at him as they should for he carried a little cloud
of fear about with him.

Only one brave and beautiful boy of ten named
Andy from Salinas ever crossed the old Chinaman.
Andy was visiting in Monterey and he saw the old man
and knew he must shout at him if only to keep his
self-respect, but even Andy, brave as he was, felt the
little cloud of fear. Andy watched him go by evening
after evening while his duty and his terror wrestled.
And then one evening Andy braced himself and
marched behind the old man singing in a shrill fal-
setto, "Ching-Chong Chinaman sitting on a rail—'Long
came a white man an' chopped off his tail."

The old man stopped and turned. Andy stopped.
The deep-brown eyes looked at Andy and the thin
corded lips moved. What happened then Andy was
never able either to explain or to forget. For the eyes
spread out until there was no Chinaman. And then it
was one eye—one huge brown eye as big as a church
door. Andy looked through the shiny transparent

brown door and through it he saw a lonely countryside, flat for miles but ending against a row of fantastic mountains shaped like cows' and dogs' heads and tents and mushrooms. There was low coarse grass on the plain and here and there a little mound. And a small animal like a woodchuck sat on each mound. And the loneliness—the desolate cold aloneness of the landscape made Andy whimper because there wasn't anybody at all in the world and he was left. Andy shut his eyes so he wouldn't have to see it any more and when he opened them, he was in Cannery Row and the old Chinaman was just flap-flapping between Western Biological and the Hediondo Cannery. Andy was the only boy who ever did that and he never did it again.

5

Western Biological was
right across the street and facing the vacant lot. Lee
Chong's grocery was on its catty-corner right and
Dora's Bear Flag Restaurant was on its catty-corner
left. Western Biological deals in strange and beautiful
wares. It sells the lovely animals of the sea, the
sponges, tunicates, anemones, the stars and buttle-
stars, and sun stars, the bivalves, barnacles, the
worms and shells, the fabulous and multiform little
brothers, the living moving flowers of the sea, nudibranchs and tectibranchs, the spiked and nobbed and
needly urchins, the crabs and demi-crabs, the little
dragons, the snapping shrimps, and ghost shrimps so
transparent that they hardly throw a shadow. And
Western Biological sells bugs and snails and spiders,
and rattlesnakes, and rats, and honey bees and gila
monsters. These are all for sale. Then there are little
unborn humans, some whole and others sliced thin
and mounted on slides. And for students there are
sharks with the blood drained out and yellow and blue

color substituted in veins and arteries, so that you may
follow the systems with a scapel. And there are cats
with colored veins and arteries, and frogs the same.
You can order anything living from Western Biological
and sooner or later you will get it.

It is a low building facing the street. The basement
is the storeroom with shelves, shelves clear to the
ceiling loaded with jars of preserved animals. And in
the basement is a sink and instruments for embalming
and for injecting. Then you go through the backyard to
a covered shed on piles over the ocean and here are
the tanks for the larger animals, the sharks and rays
and octopi, each in their concrete tanks. There is a
stairway up the front of the building and a door that
opens into an office where there is a desk piled high
with unopened mail, filing cabinets, and a safe with
the door propped open. Once the safe got locked by
mistake and no one knew the combination. And in the
safe was an open can of sardines and a piece of Roque-
fort cheese. Before the combination could be sent by
the maker of the lock, there was trouble in the safe. It
was then that Doc devised a method for getting re-
venge on a bank if anyone should ever want to. "Rent
a safety deposit box," he said, "then deposit in it one
whole fresh salmon and go away for six months." After
the trouble with the safe, it was not permitted to keep
food there any more. It is kept in the filing cabinets.
Behind the office is a room where in aquaria are many
living animals; there also are the microscopes and the
slides and the drug cabinets, the cases of laboratory
glass, the work benches and little motors, the chemi-
cals. From this room come smells—formaline, and dry

starfish, and sea water and menthol, carbolic acid and
acetic acid, smell of brown wrapping paper and straw
and rope, smell of chloroform and ether, smell of
ozone from the motors, smell of fine steel and thin
lubricant from the microscopes, smell of banana oil
and rubber tubing, smell of drying wool socks and
boots, sharp pungent smell of rattlesnakes, and musty
frightening smell of rats. And through the back door
comes the smell of kelp and barnacles when the tide is
out and the smell of salt and spray when the tide is in.

To the left the office opens into a library. The walls
are bookcases to the ceiling, boxes of pamphlets and
separates, books of all kinds, dictionaries, encyclope-
dias, poetry, plays. A great phonograph stands against
the wall with hundreds of records lined up beside it.
Under the window is a redwood bed and on the walls
and to the bookcases are pinned reproductions of Dau-
miers, and Graham, Titian, and Leonardo and Pi-
casso, Dali and George Grosz, pinned here and there
at eye level so that you can look at them if you want
to. There are chairs and benches in this little room
and of course the bed. As many as forty people have
been here at one time.

Behind this library or music room, or whatever you
want to call it, is the kitchen, a narrow chamber with a
gas stove, a water heater, and a sink. But whereas
some food is kept in the filing cabinets in the office,
dishes and cooking fat and vegetables are kept in
glass-fronted sectional bookcases in the kitchen. No
whimsy dictated this. It just happened. From the ceiling of the kitchen hang pieces of bacon, and salami,
and black bêche-de-mer. Behind the kitchen is a toilet

and a shower. The toilet leaked for five years until a clever and handsome guest fixed it with a piece of chewing gum.

Doc is the owner and operator of the Western Biological Laboratory. Doc is rather small, deceptively small, for he is wiry and very strong and when passionate anger comes on him he can be very fierce. He wears a beard and his face is half Christ and half satyr and his face tells the truth. It is said that he has helped many a girl out of one trouble and into another. Doc has the hands of a brain surgeon, and a cool warm mind. Doc tips his hat to dogs as he drives by and the dogs look up and smile at him. He can kill anything for need but he could not even hurt a feeling for pleasure. He has one great fear—that of getting his head wet, so that summer or winter he ordinarily wears a rain hat. He will wade in a tide pool up to the chest without feeling damp, but a drop of rain water on his head makes him panicky.

Over a period of years Doc dug himself into Cannery Row to an extent not even he suspected. He became the fountain of philosophy and science and art. In the laboratory the girls from Dora's heard the Plain Songs and Gregorian music for the first time. Lee Chong listened while Li Po was read to him in English. Henri the painter heard for the first time the Book of the Dead and was so moved that he changed his medium. Henri had been painting with glue, iron rust, and colored chicken feathers but he changed and his next four paintings were done entirely with different kinds of nutshells. Doc would listen to any kind of nonsense and change it for you to a kind of wisdom. His mind had no horizon—and his sympathy had no warp. He could talk to children, telling them very profound things so that they understood. He lived in a world of wonders, of excitement. He was concupiscent as a rabbit and gentle as hell. Everyone who knew him was indebted to him. And everyone who thought of him thought next, "I really must do something nice for Doc."

6

Doc was collecting marine
animals in the Great Tide Pool on the tip of the Penin-
sula. It is a fabulous place: when the tide is in, a
wave-churned basin, creamy with foam, whipped by
the combers that roll in from the whistling buoy on the
reef. But when the tide goes out the little water world
becomes quiet and lovely. The sea is very clear and
the bottom becomes fantastic with hurrying, fighting,
feeding, breeding animals. Crabs rush from frond to
frond of the waving algae. Starfish squat over mussels
and limpets, attach their million little suckers and
then slowly lift with incredible power until the prey is
broken from the rock. And then the starfish stomach
comes out and envelops its food. Orange and speckled
and fluted nudibranchs slide gracefully over the rocks,
their skirts waving like the dresses of Spanish dancers.
And black eels poke their heads out of crevices and
wait for prey. The snapping shrimps with their trigger
claws pop loudly. The lovely, colored world is glassed
over. Hermit crabs like frantic children scamper on
the bottom sand. And now one, finding an empty snail

shell he likes better than his own, creeps out, expos-
ing his soft body to the enemy for a moment, and then
pops into the new shell. A wave breaks over the barrier, and churns the glassy water for a moment and
mixes bubbles into the pool, and then it clears and is
tranquil and lovely and murderous again. Here a crab
tears a leg from his brother. The anemones expand
like soft and brilliant flowers, inviting any tired and
perplexed animal to lie for a moment in their arms,
and when some small crab or little tide-pool Johnnie
accepts the green and purple invitation, the petals
whip in, the stinging cells shoot tiny narcotic needles
into the prey and it grows weak and perhaps sleepy
while the searing caustic digestive acids melt its body
down.

Then the creeping murderer, the octopus, steals
out, slowly, softly, moving like a gray mist, pretending
now to be a bit of weed, now a rock, now a lump of
decaying meat while its evil goat eyes watch coldly. It
oozes and flows toward a feeding crab, and as it comes
close its yellow eyes burn and its body turns rosy with
the pulsing color of anticipation and rage. Then suddenly it runs lightly on the tips of its arms, as fero-
ciously as a charging cat. It leaps savagely on the
crab, there is a puff of black fluid, and the struggling
mass is obscured in the sepia cloud while the octopus
murders the crab. On the exposed rocks out of water,
the barnacles bubble behind their closed doors and the
limpets dry out. And down to the rocks come the black
flies to eat anything they can find. The sharp smell of
iodine from the algae, and the lime smell of calcareous
bodies and the smell of powerful protean, smell of
sperm and ova fill the air. On the exposed rocks the

starfish emit semen and eggs from between their rays. The smells of life and richness, of death and digestion, of decay and birth, burden the air. And salt spray blows in from the barrier where the ocean waits for its rising-tide strength to permit it back into the Great Tide Pool again. And on the reef the whistling buoy bellows like a sad and patient bull.

In the pool Doc and Hazel worked together. Hazel lived in the Palace Flophouse with Mack and the boys. Hazel got his name in as haphazard a way as his life was ever afterward. His worried mother had had seven children in eight years. Hazel was the eighth, and his mother became confused about his sex when he was born. She was tired and run down anyway from trying to feed and clothe seven children and their father. She had tried every possible way of making money—paper flowers, mushrooms at home, rabbits for meat and fur—while her husband from a canvas chair gave her every help his advice and reasoning and criticism could offer. She had a great aunt named Hazel who was reputed to carry life insurance. The eighth child was named Hazel before the mother got it through her head that Hazel was a boy and by that time she was used to the name and never bothered to change it. Hazel grew up—did four years in grammar school, four years in reform school, and didn't learn anything in either place. Reform schools are supposed to teach viciousness and criminality but Hazel didn't pay enough attention. He came out of reform school as innocent of viciousness as he was of fractions and long division. Hazel loved to hear conversation but he didn't listen to words—just to the tone of conversation. He asked questions, not to hear the answers but simply to continue the flow. He was twenty-six—dark-haired and pleasant, strong, willing, and loyal. Quite often he went collecting with Doc and he was very good at it once he knew what was wanted. His fingers could creep like an octopus, could grab and hold like an anemone. He was sure-footed on the slippery rocks and he loved the hunt. Doc wore his rain hat and high rubber boots as he worked but Hazel sloshed about in tennis shoes and blue jeans. They were collecting starfish. Doc had an order for three hundred.

Hazel picked a nobby purplish starfish from the bottom of the pool and popped it into his nearly full gunny sack. "I wonder what they do with them," he said.

"Do with what?" Doc asked.

"The starfish," said Hazel. "You sell 'em. You'll send out a barrel of 'em. What do the guys do with 'em? You can't eat 'em."

"They study them," said Doc patiently and he remembered that he had answered this question for Hazel dozens of times before. But Doc had one mental habit he could not get over. When anyone asked a question, Doc thought he wanted to know the answer. That was the way with Doc. *He* never asked unless he wanted to know and he could not conceive of the brain that would ask without wanting to know. But Hazel, who simply wanted to hear talk, had developed a system of making the answer to one question the basis of another. It kept conversation going.

"What do they find to study?" Hazel continued. "They're just starfish. There's millions of 'em around. I could get you a million of 'em."

"They're complicated and interesting animals," Doc

said a little defensively. "Besides, these are going to the Middle West to Northwestern University."

Hazel used his trick. "They got no starfish there?"

"They got no ocean there," said Doc.

"Oh!" said Hazel and he cast frantically about for a peg to hang a new question on. He hated to have a conversation die out like this. He wasn't quick enough. While he was looking for a question Doc asked one. Hazel hated that, it meant casting about in his mind for an answer and casting about in Hazel's mind was like wandering alone in a deserted museum. Hazel's mind was choked with uncatalogued exhibits. He never forgot anything but he never bothered to arrange his memories. Everything was thrown together like fishing tackle in the bottom of a rowboat, hooks and sinkers and line and lures and gaffs all snarled up.

Doc asked, "How are things going up at the Palace?"

Hazel ran his fingers through his dark hair and he peered into the clutter of his mind. "Pretty good," he said. "That fellow Gay is moving in with us I guess. His wife hits him pretty bad. He don't mind that when he's awake but she waits 'til he gets to sleep and then hits him. He hates that. He has to wake up and beat her up and then when he goes back to sleep she hits him again. He don't get any rest so he's moving in with us."

"That's a new one," said Doc. "She used to swear out a warrant and put him in jail."

"Yeah!" said Hazel. "But that was before they built the new jail in Salinas. Used to be thirty days and Gay was pretty hot to get out, but this new jail—radio in the tank and good bunks and the sheriff's a nice fel-

low. Gay gets in there and he don't want to come out.
He likes it so much his wife won't get him arrested any
more. So she figured out this hitting him while he's
asleep. It's nerve racking, he says. And you know as
good as me—Gay never did take any pleasure beating
her up. He only done it to keep his self-respect. But
he gets tired of it. I guess he'll be with us now."

Doc straightened up. The waves were beginning to
break over the barrier of the Great Tide Pool. The tide
was coming in and little rivers from the sea had begun
to flow over the rocks. The wind blew freshly in from
the whistling buoy and the barking of sea lions came
from around the point. Doc pushed his rain hat on the
back of his head. "We've got enough starfish," he said
and then went on, "Look, Hazel, I know you've got six
or seven undersized abalones in the bottom of your
sack. If we get stopped by a game warden, you're
going to say they're mine, on my permit—aren't you?"

"Well—hell," said Hazel.

"Look," Doc said kindly. "Suppose I get an order
for abalones and maybe the game warden thinks I'm
using my collecting permit too often. Suppose he
thinks I'm eating them."

"Well—hell," said Hazel.

"It's like the industrial alcohol board. They've got
suspicious minds. They always think I'm drinking the
alcohol. They think that about everyone."

"Well, ain't you?"

"Not much of it," said Doc. "That stuff they put in
it tastes terrible and it's a big job to redistill it."

"That stuff ain't so bad," said Hazel. "Me and Mack
had a snort of it the other day. What is it they put in?"

Doc was about to answer when he saw it was Hazel's trick again. "Let's get moving," he said. He hoisted his sack of starfish on his shoulder. And he had forgotten the illegal abalones in the bottom of Hazel's sack.

Hazel followed him up out of the tide pool and up the slippery trail to solid ground. The little crabs scampered and skittered out of their way. Hazel felt that he had better cement the grave over the topic of the abalones.

"That painter guy came back to the Palace," he offered.

"Yes?" said Doc.

"Yeah! You see, he done all our pictures in chicken feathers and now he says he got to do them all over again with nutshells. He says he changed his—his med—medium."

Doc chuckled. "He still building his boat?"

"Sure," said Hazel. "He's got it all changed around. New kind of a boat. I guess he'll take it apart and change it. Doc—is he nuts?"

Doc swung his heavy sack of starfish to the ground and stood panting a little. "Nuts?" he asked. "Oh, yes, I guess so. Nuts about the same amount we are, only in a different way."

Such a thing had never occurred to Hazel. He looked upon himself as a crystal pool of clarity and on his life as a troubled glass of misunderstood virtue. Doc's last statement had outraged him a little. "But that boat—" he cried. "He's been building that boat for seven years that I know of. The blocks rotted out and he made concrete blocks. Every time he gets it nearly finished he changes it and starts over again. I think he's nuts. Seven years on a boat."

Doc was sitting on the ground pulling off his rubber boots. "You don't understand," he said gently. "Henri loves boats but he's afraid of the ocean."

"What's he want a boat for then?" Hazel demanded.

"He likes boats," said Doc. "But suppose he finishes his boat. Once it's finished people will say, 'Why don't you put it in the water?' Then if he puts it in the water, he'll have to go out in it, and he hates the water. So you see, he never finishes the boat—so he doesn't ever have to launch it."

Hazel had followed this reasoning to a certain point but he abandoned it before it was resolved, not only abandoned it but searched for some way to change the subject. "I think he's nuts," he said lamely.

On the black earth on which the ice plants bloomed, hundreds of black stink bugs crawled. And many of them stuck their tails up in the air. "Look at all them stink bugs," Hazel remarked, grateful to the bugs for being there.

"They're interesting," said Doc.

"Well, what they got their asses up in the air for?"

Doc rolled up his wool socks and put them in the rubber boots and from his pocket he brought out dry socks and a pair of thin moccasins. "I don't know why," he said. "I looked them up recently—they're very common animals and one of the commonest things they do is put their tails up in the air. And in all the books there isn't one mention of the fact that they put their tails up in the air or why."

Hazel turned one of the stink bugs over with the toe of his wet tennis shoe and the shining black beetle strove madly with floundering legs to get upright again. "Well, why do *you* think they do it?"

"I think they're praying," said Doc.

"What!" Hazel was shocked.

"The remarkable thing," said Doc, "isn't that they put their tails up in the air—the really incredibly remarkable thing is that we find it remarkable. We can only use ourselves as yardsticks. If we did something as inexplicable and strange we'd probably be praying—so maybe they're praying."

"Let's get the hell out of here," said Hazel.

7

The Palace Flophouse was no sudden development. Indeed when Mack and Hazel and Eddie and Hughie and Jones moved into it, they looked upon it as little more than shelter from the wind and the rain, as a place to go when everything else had closed or when their welcome was thin and sere with overuse. Then the Palace was only a long bare room, lit dimly by two small windows, walled with unpainted wood smelling strongly of fish meal. They had not loved it then. But Mack knew that some kind of organization was necessary particularly among such a group of ravening individualists.

A training army which has not been equipped with guns and artillery and tanks uses artificial guns and masquerading trucks to simulate its destructive panoply—and its toughening soldiers get used to field guns by handling logs on wheels.

Mack, with a piece of chalk, drew five oblongs on the floor, each seven feet long and four feet wide, and in each square he wrote a name. These were the simulated beds. Each man had property rights inviolable in

his space. He could legally fight a man who en-
croached on his square. The rest of the room was
property common to all. That was in the first days
when Mack and the boys sat on the floor, played cards
hunkered down, and slept on the hard boards. Perhaps, save for an accident of weather, they might always have lived that way. However, an unprecedented
rainfall which went on for over a month changed all
that. House-ridden, the boys grew tired of squatting on
the floor. Their eyes became outraged by the bare
board walls. Because it sheltered them the house grew
dear to them. And it had the charm of never knowing
the entrance of an outraged landlord. For Lee Chong
never came near it. Then one afternoon Hughie came
in with an army cot which had a torn canvas. He spent
two hours sewing up the rip with fishing line. And that
night the others lying on the floor in their squares
watched Hughie ooze gracefully into his cot—they
heard him sigh with abysmal comfort and he was
asleep and snoring before anyone else.

The next day Mack puffed up the hill carrying a
rusty set of springs he had found on a scrap-iron
dump. The apathy was broken then. The boys outdid
one another in beautifying the Palace Flophouse until
after a few months it was, if anything, overfurnished.
There were old carpets on the floor, chairs with and
without seats. Mack had a wicker chaise longue
painted bright red. There were tables, a grandfather
clock without dial face or works. The walls were white-
washed which made it almost light and airy. Pictures
began to appear—mostly calendars showing improb-
able luscious blondes holding bottles of Coca-Cola.
Henri had contributed two pieces from his chicken-

feather period. A bundle of gilded cattails stood in one corner and a sheaf of peacock feathers was nailed to the wall beside the grandfather clock.

They were some time acquiring a stove and when they did find what they wanted, a silver-scrolled monster with floriated warming ovens and a front like a nickel-plated tulip garden, they had trouble getting it. It was too big to steal and its owner refused to part with it to the sick widow with eight children whom Mack invented and patronized in the same moment. The owner wanted a dollar and a half and didn't come down to eighty cents for three days. The boys closed at eighty cents and gave him an I.O.U. which he probably still has. This transaction took place in Seaside and the stove weighed three hundred pounds. Mack and Hughie exhausted every possibility of haulage for ten days and only when they realized that no one was going to take this stove home for them did they begin to carry it. It took them three days to carry it to Cannery Row, a distance of five miles, and they camped beside it at night. But once installed in the Palace Flophouse it was the glory and the hearth and the center. Its nickel flowers and foliage shone with a cheery light. It was the gold tooth of the Palace. Fired up, it warmed the big room. Its oven was wonderful and you could fry an egg on its shiny black lids.

With the great stove came pride, and with pride, the Palace became home. Eddie planted morning glories to run over the door and Hazel acquired some rather rare fuchsia bushes planted in five-gallon cans which made the entrance formal and a little cluttered. Mack and the boys loved the Palace and they even cleaned it a little sometimes. In their minds they sneered at unsettled people who had no house to go to and occasionally in their pride they brought a guest home for a day or two.

Eddie was understudy bartender at La Ida. He filled in when Whitey the regular bartender was sick, which was as often as Whitey could get away with it. Every time Eddie filled in, a few bottles disappeared, so he couldn't fill in too often. But Whitey liked to have Eddie take his place because he was convinced, and correctly, that Eddie was one man who wouldn't try to keep his job permanently. Almost anyone could have trusted Eddie to this extent. Eddie didn't have to remove much liquor. He kept a gallon jug under the bar and in the mouth of the jug there was a funnel. Anything left in the glasses Eddie poured into the funnel before he washed the glasses. If an argument or a song were going on at La Ida, or late at night when good fellowship had reached its logical conclusion, Eddie poured glasses half or two-thirds full into the funnel. The resulting punch which he took back to the Palace was always interesting and sometimes surprising. The mixture of rye, beer, bourbon, scotch, wine, rum and gin was fairly constant, but now and then some effete customer would order a stinger or an anisette or a curaçao and these little touches gave a distinct character to the punch. It was Eddie's habit always to shake a little angostura into the jug just before he left. On a good night Eddie got three-quarters of a gallon. It was a source of satisfaction to him that nobody was out anything. He had observed that a man got just as drunk on half a glass as on a whole one, that is, if he was in the mood to get drunk at all.

Eddie was a very desirable inhabitant of the Palace

Flophouse. The others never asked him to help with the housecleaning and once Hazel washed four pairs of Eddie's socks.

Now on the afternoon when Hazel was out collecting with Doc in the Great Tide Pool, the boys were sitting around in the Palace sipping the result of Eddie's latest contribution. Gay was there too, the latest member of the group. Eddie sipped speculatively from his glass and smacked his lips. "It's funny how you get a run," he said. "Take last night. There was at least ten guys ordered Manhattans. Sometimes maybe you don't get two calls for a Manhattan in a month. It's the grenadine gives the stuff that taste."

Mack tasted his—a big taste—and refilled his glass. "Yes," he said somberly, "it's little things make the difference." He looked about to see how this gem had set with the others.

Only Gay got the full impact. "Sure is," he said. "Does—"

"Where's Hazel today?" Mack asked.

Jones said, "Hazel went out with Doc to get some starfish."

Mack nodded his head soberly. "That Doc is a hell of a nice fella," he said. "He'll give you a quarter any time. When I cut myself he put on a new bandage every day. A hell of a nice fella."

The others nodded in profound agreement.

"I been wondering for a long time," Mack continued, "what we could do for him—something nice. Something he'd like."

"He'd like a dame," said Hughie.

"He's got three four dames," said Jones. "You can always tell—when he pulls them front curtains closed and when he plays that kind of church music on the phonograph."

Mack said reprovingly to Hughie, "Just because he doesn't run no dame naked through the streets in the daytime, you think Doc's celebrate."

"What's celebrate?" Eddie asked.

"That's when you can't get no dame," said Mack.

"I thought it was a kind of a party," said Jones.

A silence fell on the room. Mack shifted in his chaise longue. Hughie let the front legs of his chair down on the floor. They looked into space and then they all looked at Mack. Mack said, "Hum!"

Eddie said, "What kind of a party you think Doc'd like?"

"What other kind is there?" said Jones.

Mack mused, "Doc wouldn't like this stuff from the winin' jug."

"How do you know?" Hughie demanded. "You never offered him none."

"Oh, I know," said Mack. "He's been to college. Once I seen a dame in a fur coat go in there. Never did see her come out. It was two o'clock the last I looked—and that church music goin'. No—you couldn't offer him none of this." He filled his glass again.

"This tastes pretty nice after the third glass," Hughie said loyally.

"No," said Mack. "Not for Doc. Have to be whis-key—the real thing."

"He likes beer," said Jones. "He's all the time go-ing over to Lee's for beer—sometimes in the middle of the night."

Mack said, "I figure when you buy beer, you're

buying too much tare. Take 8 percent beer—why you're spending your dough for 92 percent water and color and hops and stuff like that. Eddie," he added, "you think you could get four five bottles of whiskey at La Ida next time Whitey's sick?"

"Sure," said Eddie. "Sure I could get it but that'd be the end—no more golden eggs. I think Johnnie's suspicious anyways. Other day he says, 'I smell a mouse named Eddie.' I was gonna lay low and only bring the jug for a while."

"Yeah!" said Jones. "Don't you lose that job. If something happened to Whitey, you could fall right in there for a week or so 'til they got somebody else. I guess if we're goin' to give a party for Doc, we got to buy the whiskey. How much is whiskey a gallon?"

"I don't know," said Hughie. "I never get more than a half pint at a time myself—at one time that is. I figure you get a quart and right away you got friends. But you get a half pint and you can drink it in the lot before—well before you got a lot of folks around."

"It's going to take dough to give Doc a party," said Mack. "If we're going to give him a party at all it ought to be a good one. Should have a big cake. I wonder when is his birthday?"

"Don't need a birthday for a party," said Jones.

"No—but it's nice," said Mack. "I figure it would take ten or twelve bucks to give Doc a party you wouldn't be ashamed of."

They looked at one another speculatively. Hughie suggested, "The Hediondo Cannery is hiring guys."

"No," said Mack quickly. "We got good reputations and we don't want to spoil them. Every one of us keeps a job for a month or more when we take one. That's

why we can always get a job when we need one. S'pose
we take a job for a day or so—why we'll lose our
reputation for sticking. Then if we needed a job there
wouldn't nobody have us." The rest nodded quick
agreement.

"I figure I'm gonna work a couple of months—No-
vember and part of December," said Jones. "Makes it
nice to have money around Christmas. We could cook a
turkey this year."

"By God, we could," said Mack. "I know a place up
Carmel Valley where there's fifteen hundred in one
flock."

"Valley," said Hughie. "You know I used to collect
stuff up the Valley for Doc, turtles and crayfish and
frogs. Got a nickel apiece for frogs."

"Me, too," said Gay. "I got five hundred frogs one
time."

"If Doc needs frogs it's a setup," said Mack. "We
could go up the Carmel River and have a little outing
and we wouldn't tell Doc what it was for and then we'd
give him one hell of a party."

A quiet excitement grew in the Palace Flophouse.
"Gay," said Mack, "take a look out the door and see if
Doc's car is in front of his place."

Gat set down his glass and looked out. "Not yet," he
said.

"Well, he ought to be back any minute," said
Mack. "Now here's how we'll go about it. . . ."

8

In April 1932 the boiler at the Hediondo Cannery blew a tube for the third time in two weeks and the board of directors consisting of Mr. Randolph and a stenographer decided that it would be cheaper to buy a new boiler than to have to shut down so often. In time the new boiler arrived and the old one was moved into the vacant lot between Lee Chong's and the Bear Flag Restaurant where it was set on blocks to await an inspiration on Mr. Randolph's part on how to make some money out of it. Gradually the plant engineer removed the tubing to use to patch other outworn equipment at the Hediondo. The boiler looked like an old-fashioned locomotive without wheels. It had a big door in the center of its nose and a low fire door. Gradually it became red and soft with rust and gradually the mallow weeds grew up around it and the flaking rust fed the weeds. Flowering myrtle crept up its sides and the wild anise perfumed the air about it. Then someone threw out a datura root and the thick fleshy tree grew up and the great white bells hung down over the boiler door and at night the flowers smelled of love and excitement, an incredibly sweet and moving odor.

In 1935 Mr. and Mrs. Sam Malloy moved into the boiler. The tubing was all gone now and it was a roomy, dry, and safe apartment. True, if you came in through the fire door you had to get down on your hands and knees, but once in there was head room in the middle and you couldn't want a dryer, warmer place to stay. They shagged a mattress through the fire door and settled down. Mr. Malloy was happy and contented there and for quite a long time so was Mrs. Malloy.

Below the boiler on the hill there were numbers of large pipes also abandoned by the Hediondo. Toward the end of 1937 there was a great catch of fish and the canneries were working full time and a housing shortage occurred. Then it was that Mr. Malloy took to renting the larger pipes as sleeping quarters for single men at a very nominal fee. With a piece of tar paper over one end and a square of carpet over the other, they made comfortable bedrooms, although men used to sleeping curled up had to change their habits or move out. There were those too who claimed that their snores echoing back from the pipes woke them up. But on the whole Mr. Malloy did a steady small business and was happy.

Mrs. Malloy had been contented until her husband became a landlord and then she began to change. First it was a rug, then a washtub, then a lamp with a colored silk shade. Finally she came into the boiler on her hands and knees one day and she stood up and said a little breathlessly, "Holman's are having a sale of curtains. Real lace curtains and edges of blue and pink—$1.98 a set with curtain rods thrown in."

Mr. Malloy sat up on the mattress. "Curtains?" he demanded. "What in God's name do you want curtains for?"

"I like things nice," said Mrs. Malloy. "I always did like to have things nice for you," and her lower lip began to tremble.

"But, darling," Sam Malloy cried, "I got nothing against curtains. I like curtains."

"Only $1.98," Mrs. Malloy quavered, "and you begrutch me $1.98," and she sniffed and her chest heaved.

"I don't begrutch you," said Mr. Malloy. "But, darling—for Christ's sake what are we going to do with curtains? We got no windows."

Mrs. Malloy cried and cried and Sam held her in his arms and comforted her.

"Men just don't understand how a woman feels," she sobbed. "Men just never try to put themselves in a woman's place."

And Sam lay beside her and rubbed her back for a long time before she went to sleep.

9

When Doc's car came back to the laboratory, Mack and the boys secretly watched Hazel help to carry in the sacks of starfish. In a few minutes Hazel came damply up the chicken walk to the Palace. His jeans were wet with sea water to the thighs and where it was drying the white salt rings were forming. He sat heavily in the patent rocker that was his and shucked off his wet tennis shoes.

Mack asked, "How is Doc feeling?"

"Fine," said Hazel. "You can't understand a word he says. Know what he said about stink bugs? No—I better not tell you."

"He seem in a nice friendly mood?" Mack asked.

"Sure," said Hazel. "We got two three hundred starfish. He's all right."

"I wonder if we better all go over?" Mack asked himself and he answered himself, "No I guess it would be better if one went alone. It might get him mixed up if we all went."

"What is this?" Hazel asked.

"We got plans," said Mack. "I'll go myself so as not to startle him. You guys stay here and wait. I'll come back in a few minutes."

Mack went out and he teetered down the chicken walk and across the track. Mr. Malloy was sitting on a brick in front of his boiler.

"How are you, Sam?" Mack asked.

"Pretty good."

"How's the missus?"

"Pretty good," said Mr. Malloy. "You know any kind of glue that you can stick cloth to iron?"

Ordinarily Mack would have thrown himself headlong into this problem but now he was not to be deflected. "No," he said.

He went across the vacant lot, crossed the street and entered the basement of the laboratory.

Doc had his hat off now since there was practically no chance of getting his head wet unless a pipe broke. He was busy removing the starfish from the wet sacks and arranging them on the cool concrete floor. The starfish were twisted and knotted up for a starfish loves to hang onto something and for an hour these had found only each other. Doc arranged them in long lines and very slowly they straightened out until they lay in symmetrical stars on the concrete floor. Doc's pointed brown beard was damp with perspiration as he worked. He looked up a little nervously as Mack entered. It was not that trouble always came in with Mack but something always entered with him.

"Hiya, Doc?" said Mack.

"All right," said Doc uneasily.

"Hear about Phyllis Mae over at the Bear Flag? She

hit a drunk and got his tooth in her fist and it's in-
fected clear to the elbow. She showed me the tooth. It
was out of a plate. Is a false tooth poison, Doc?"

"I guess everything that comes out of the human
mouth is poison," said Doc warningfully. "Has she got
a doctor?"

"The bouncer fixed her up," said Mack.

"I'll take her some sulfa," said Doc, and he waited
for the storm to break. He knew Mack had come for
something and Mack knew he knew it.

Mack said, "Doc, you got any need for any kind of
animals now?"

Doc sighed with relief. "Why?" he asked guardedly.

Mack became open and confidential. "I'll tell you,
Doc. I and the boys got to get some dough—we simply
got to. It's for a good purpose, you might say a worthy
cause."

"Phyllis Mae's arm?"

Mack saw the chance, weighed it and gave it up.
"Well—no," he said. "It's more important than that.
You can't kill a whore. No—this is different. I and the
boys thought if you needed something why we'd get it
for you and that way we could make a little piece of
change."

It seemed simple and innocent. Doc laid down four
more starfish in lines. "I could use three or four hundred frogs," he said. "I'd get them myself but I've got
to go down to La Jolla tonight. There's a good tide
tomorrow and I have to get some octopi."

"Same price for frogs?" Mack asked. "Five cents
apiece?"

"Same price," said Doc.

Mack was jovial. "Don't you worry about frogs, Doc," he said. "We'll get you all the frogs you want. You just rest easy about frogs. Why we can get them right up Carmel River. I know a place."

"Good," said Doc. "I'll take all you get but I need about three hundred."

"Just you rest easy, Doc. Don't you lose no sleep about it. You'll get your frogs, maybe seven eight hundred." He put the Doc at his ease about frogs and then a little cloud crossed Mack's face. "Doc," he said, "any chance of using your car to go up the Valley?"

"No," said Doc. "I told you. I have to drive to La Jolla tonight to make tomorrow's tide."

"Oh," said Mack dispiritedly. "Oh. Well, don't you worry about it, Doc. Maybe we can get Lee Chong's old truck." And then his face fell a little further. "Doc," he said, "on a business deal like this, would you advance two or three bucks for gasoline? I know Lee Chong won't give us gas."

"No," said Doc. He had fallen into this before. Once he had financed Gay to go for turtles. He financed him for two weeks and at the end of that time Gay was in jail on his wife's charge and he never did go for turtles.

"Well, maybe we can't go then," said Mack sadly.

Now Doc really needed the frogs. He tried to work out some method which was business and not philanthropy. "I'll tell you what I'll do," he said. "I'll give you a note to my gas station so you can get ten gallons of gas. How will that be?"

Mack smiled. "Fine," he said. "That will work out just fine. I and the boys will get an early start tomorrow. Time you get back from the south, we'll have more damn frogs than you ever seen in your life."

Doc went to the labeling desk and wrote a note to Red Williams at the gas station, authorizing the issue of ten gallons of gasoline to Mack. "Here you are," he said.

Mack was smiling broadly. "Doc," he said, "you can get to sleep tonight and not even give frogs a thought. We'll have piss pots full of them by the time you get back."

Doc watched him go a little uneasily. Doc's dealings with Mack and the boys had always been interesting but rarely had they been profitable to Doc. He remembered ruefully the time Mack sold him fifteen tom cats and by night the owners came and got every one. "Mack," he had asked, "why all tom cats?"

Mack said, "Doc, it's my own invention but I'll tell you because you're a good friend. You make a big wire trap and then you don't use bait. You use—well—you use a lady cat. Catch every God damn tom cat in the country that way."

From the laboratory Mack crossed the street and went through the swinging screen doors into Lee Chong's grocery. Mrs. Lee was cutting bacon on the big butcher's block. A Lee cousin primped up slightly wilted heads of lettuce the way a girl primps a loose finger wave. A cat lay asleep on a big pile of oranges. Lee Chong stood in his usual place back of the cigar counter and in front of the liquor shelves. His tapping finger on the change mat speeded up a little when Mack came in.

Mack wasted no time in sparring. "Lee," he said,

"Doc over there's got a problem. He's got a big order for frogs from the New York Museum. Means a lot to Doc. Besides the dough there's a lot of credit getting an order like that. Doc's got to go south and I and the boys said we'd help him out. I think a guy's friends ought to help him out of a hole when they can, especially a nice guy like Doc. Why I bet he spends sixty seventy dollars a month with you."

Lee Chong remained silent and watchful. His fat finger barely moved on the change mat but it flicked slightly like a tense cat's tail.

Mack plunged into his thesis. "Will you let us take your old truck to go up Carmel Valley for frogs for Doc—for good old Doc?"

Lee Chong smiled in triumph. "Tluck no good," he said. "Bloke down."

This staggered Mack for a moment but he recovered. He spread the order for gasoline on the cigar counter. "Look!" he said. "Doc needs them frogs. He give me this order for gas to get them. I can't let Doc down. Now Gay is a good mechanic. If he fixes your truck and puts it in good shape, will you let us take it?"

Lee put back his head so that he could see Mack through his half-glasses. There didn't seem to be anything wrong with the proposition. The truck really wouldn't run. Gay really was a good mechanic and the order for gasoline was definite evidence of good faith.

"How long you be gone?" Lee asked.

"Maybe half a day, maybe a whole day. Just 'til we get the frogs."

Lee was worried but he couldn't see any way out.

The dangers were all there and Lee knew all of them. "Okay," said Lee.

"Good," said Mack. "I knew Doc could depend on you. I'll get Gay right to work on that truck." He turned about to leave. "By the way," he said. "Doc's paying us five cents apiece for those frogs. We're going to get seven or eight hundred. How about taking a pint of Old Tennis Shoes just 'til we can get back with the frogs?"

"No!" said Lee Chong.

10

Frankie began coming to Western Biological when he was eleven years old. For a week or so he just stood outside the basement door and looked in. Then one day he stood inside the door. Ten days later he was in the basement. He had very large eyes and his hair was a dark wiry dirty shock. His hands were filthy. He picked up a piece of excelsior and put it in a garbage can and then he looked at Doc where he worked labeling specimen bottles containing purple Velella. Finally Frankie got to the work bench and he put his dirty fingers on the bench. It took Frankie three weeks to get that far and he was ready to bolt every instant of the time.

Finally one day Doc spoke to him. "What's your name, son?"

"Frankie."

"Where do you live?"

"Up there," a gesture up the hill.

"Why aren't you in school?"

"I don't go to school."

"Why not?"

"They don't want me there."

"Your hands are dirty. Don't you ever wash?"

Frankie looked stricken and then he went to the sink and scrubbed his hands and always afterwards he scrubbed his hands almost raw every day.

And he came to the laboratory every day. It was an association without much talk. Doc by a telephone call established that what Frankie said was true. They didn't want him in school. He couldn't learn and there was something a little wrong with his coordination. There was no place for him. He wasn't an idiot, he wasn't dangerous, his parents, or parent, would not pay for his keep in an institution. Frankie didn't often sleep at the laboratory but he spent his days there. And sometimes he crawled in the excelsior crate and slept. That was probably when there was a crisis at home.

Doc asked, "Why do you come here?"

"You don't hit me or give me a nickel," said Frankie.

"Do they hit you at home?"

"There's uncles around all the time at home. Some of them hit me and tell me to get out and some of them give me a nickel and tell me to get out."

"Where's your father?"

"Dead," said Frankie vaguely.

"Where's your mother?"

"With the uncles."

Doc clipped Frankie's hair and got rid of the lice. At Lee Chong's he got him a new pair of overalls and a striped sweater and Frankie became his slave.

"I love you," he said one afternoon. "Oh, I love you."

He wanted to work in the laboratory. He swept out every day, but there was something a little wrong. He couldn't get a floor quite clean. He tried to help with grading crayfish for size. There they were in a bucket, all sizes. They were to be grouped in the big pans— laid out—all the three-inch ones together and all the four-inch ones and so forth. Frankie tried and the perspiration stood on his forehead but he couldn't do it. Size relationships just didn't get through to him.

"No," Doc would say. "Look, Frankie. Put them beside your finger like this so you'll know which ones are this long. See? This one goes from the tip of your finger to the base of your thumb. Now you just pick out another one that goes from the tip of your finger down to the same place and it will be right." Frankie tried and he couldn't do it. When Doc went upstairs Frankie crawled in the excelsior box and didn't come out all afternoon.

But Frankie was a nice, good, kind boy. He learned to light Doc's cigars and he wanted Doc to smoke all the time so he could light the cigars.

Better than anything else Frankie loved it when there were parties upstairs in the laboratory. When girls and men gathered to sit and talk, when the great phonograph played music that throbbed in his stomach and made beautiful and huge pictures form vaguely in his head, Frankie loved it. Then he crouched down in a corner behind a chair where he was hidden and could watch and listen. When there was laughter at a joke he didn't understand Frankie laughed delightedly behind his chair and when the conversation dealt with abstractions his brow furrowed and he became intent and serious.

One afternoon he did a desperate thing. There was a small party in the laboratory. Doc was in the kitchen pouring beer when Frankie appeared beside him. Frankie grabbed a glass of beer and rushed it through the door and gave it to a girl sitting in a big chair.

She took the glass and said, "Why, thank you," and she smiled at him.

And Doc coming through the door said, "Yes, Frankie is a great help to me."

Frankie couldn't forget that. He did the thing in his mind over and over, just how he had taken the glass and just how the girl sat and then her voice—"Why, thank you," and Doc—"a great help to me—Frankie is a great help to me—sure Frankie is a great help— Frankie," and Oh my God!

He knew a big party was coming because Doc bought steaks and a great deal of beer and Doc let him help clean out all the upstairs. But that was nothing, for a great plan had formed in Frankie's mind and he could see just how it would be. He went over it again and again. It was beautiful. It was perfect.

Then the party started and people came and sat in the front room, girls and young women and men.

Frankie had to wait until he had the kitchen to himself and the door closed. And it was some time before he had it so. But at last he was alone and the door was shut. He could hear the chatter of conversation and the music from the great phonograph. He worked very quietly—first the tray—then get out the glasses without breaking any. Now fill them with beer and let the foam settle a little and then fill again.

Now he was ready. He took a great breath and opened the door. The music and the talk roared

around him. Frankie picked up the tray of beer and
walked through the door. He knew how. He went
straight toward the same young woman who had
thanked him before. And then right in front of her, the
thing happened, the coordination failed, the hands
fumbled, the muscles panicked, the nerves tele-
graphed to a dead operator, the responses did not
come back. Tray and beer collapsed forward into the
young woman's lap. For a moment Frankie stood still.
And then he turned and ran.

The room was quiet. They could hear him run
downstairs, and go into the cellar. They heard a hollow
scrabbling sound—and then silence.

Doc walked quietly down the stairs and into the
cellar. Frankie was in the excelsior box burrowed
down clear to the bottom, with the pile of excelsior on
top of him. Doc could hear him whimpering there. Doc
waited for a moment and then he went quietly back
upstairs.

There wasn't a thing in the world he could do.

11

The Model T Ford truck of Lee Chong had a dignified history. In 1923 it had been a passenger car belonging to Dr. W. T. Waters. He used it for five years and sold it to an insurance man named Rattle. Mr. Rattle was not a careful man. The car he got in clean nice condition he drove like fury. Mr. Rattle drank on Saturday nights and the car suffered. The fenders were broken and bent. He was a pedal rider too and the bands had to be changed often. When Mr. Rattle embezzled a client's money and ran away to San José, he was caught with a high-hair blonde and sent up within ten days.

The body of the car was so battered that its next owner cut it in two and added a little truck bed.

The next owner took off the front of the cab and the windshield. He used it to haul squids and he liked a fresh breeze to blow in his face. His name was Francis Almones and he had a sad life, for he always made just a fraction less than he needed to live. His father had left him a little money but year by year and month by month, no matter how hard Francis worked or how careful he was, his money grew less until he just dried up and blew away.

Lee Chong got the truck in payment of a grocery bill.

By this time the truck was little more than four wheels and an engine and the engine was so crotchety and sullen and senile that it required expert care and consideration. Lee Chong did not give it these things, with the result that the truck stood in the tall grass back of the grocery most of the time with the mallows growing between its spokes. It had solid tires on its back wheels and blocks held its front wheels off the ground.

Probably any one of the boys from the Palace Flophouse could have made the truck run, for they were all competent practical mechanics, but Gay was an inspired mechanic. There is no term comparable to green thumbs to apply to such a mechanic, but there should be. For there are men who can look, listen, tap, make an adjustment, and a machine works. Indeed there are men near whom a car runs better. And such a one was Gay. His fingers on a timer or a carburetor adjustment screw were gentle and wise and sure. He could fix the delicate electric motors in the laboratory. He could have worked in the canneries all the time had he wished, for in that industry, which complains bitterly when it does not make back its total investment every year in profits, the machinery is much less important than the fiscal statement. Indeed, if you could can sardines with ledgers, the owners would have been very happy. As it was they used decrepit, struggling old horrors of machines that needed the constant attention of a man like Gay.

Mack got the boys up early. They had their coffee
and immediately moved over to the truck where it lay
among the weeds. Gay was in charge. He kicked the
blocked-up front wheels. "Go borrow a pump and get
those pumped up," he said. Then he put a stick in the
gasoline tank under the board which served as a seat.
By some miracle there was a half inch of gasoline in
the tank. Now Gay went over the most probable difficulties. He took out the coil boxes, scraped the points,
adjusted the gap, and put them back. He opened the
carburetor to see that gas came through. He pushed on
the crank to see that the whole shaft wasn't frozen and
the pistons rusted in their cylinders.

Meanwhile the pump arrived and Eddie and Jones
spelled each other on the tires.

Gay hummed, "Dum tiddy—dum tiddy," as he
worked. He removed the spark plugs and scraped the
points and bored the carbon out. Then Gay drained a
little gasoline into a can and poured some into each
cylinder before he put the spark plugs back. He
straightened up. "We're going to need a couple of dry
cells," he said. "See if Lee Chong will let us have a
couple."

Mack departed and returned almost immediately
with a universal No which was designed by Lee Chong
to cover all future requests.

Gay thought deeply. "I know where's a couple—
pretty good ones too, but I won't go get them."

"Where?" asked Mack.

"Down cellar at my house," said Gay. "They run the
front doorbell. If one of you fellas wants to kind of
edge into my cellar without my wife seeing you, they're

on top of the side stringer on the lefthand side as you go in. But for God's sake, don't let my wife catch you."

A conference elected Eddie to go and he departed. "If you get caught don't mention me," Gay called out after him. Meanwhile Gay tested the bands. The low-high pedal didn't quite touch the floor so he knew there was a little band left. The brake pedal did touch the floor so there was no brake, but the reverse pedal had lots of band left. On a Model T Ford the reverse is your margin of safety. When your brake is gone, you can use reverse as a brake. And when the low gear band is worn too thin to pull up a steep hill, why you can turn around and back up it. Gay found there was plenty of reverse and he knew everything was all right.

It was a good omen that Eddie came back with the dry cells without trouble. Mrs. Gay had been in the kitchen. Eddie could hear her walking about but she didn't hear Eddie. He was very good at such things.

Gay connected the dry cells and he advanced the gas and retarded the spark lever. "Twist her tail," he said.

He was such a wonder, Gay was—the little mechanic of God, the St. Francis of all things that turn and twist and explode, the St. Francis of coils and armatures and gears. And if at some time all the heaps of jalopies, cut-down Dusenbergs, Buicks, De Sotos and Plymouths, American Austins and Isotta-Fraschinis praise God in a great chorus—it will be largely due to Gay and his brotherhood.

One twist—one little twist and the engine caught and labored and faltered and caught again. Gay advanced the spark and reduced the gas. He switched

over to the magneto and the Ford of Lee Chong chuckled and jiggled and clattered happily as though it knew
it was working for a man who loved and understood it.

There were two small technical legal difficulties with
the truck—it had no recent license plates and it had no
lights. But the boys hung a rag permanently and acci-
dentally on the rear plate to conceal its vintage and they
dabbed the front plate with good thick mud. The equipment of the expedition was slight: some long-handled
frog nets and some gunny sacks. City hunters going out
for sport load themselves with food and liquor, but not
Mack. He presumed rightly that the country was where
food came from. Two loaves of bread and what was left
of Eddie's wining jug was all the supply. The party
clambered on the truck—Gay drove and Mack sat beside him; they bumped around the corner of Lee
Chong's and down through the lot, threading among the
pipes. Mr. Malloy waved at them from his seat by the
boiler. Gay eased across the sidewalk and down off the
curb gently because the front tires showed fabric all the
way around. With all their alacrity, it was afternoon
when they got started.

The truck eased into Red Williams' service station.
Mack got out and gave his paper to Red. He said,
"Doc was a little short of change. So if you'll put five
gallons in and just give us a buck instead of the other
five gallons, why that's what Doc wants. He had to go
south, you know. Had a big deal down there."

Red smiled good-naturedly. "You know, Mack," he
said, "Doc got to figuring if there was some kind of
loophole, and he put his finger on the same one you
did. Doc's a pretty bright fellow. So he phoned me last
night."

"Put in the whole ten gallons," said Mack. "No—wait. It'll slop around and spill. Put in five and give us five in a can—one of them sealed cans."

Red smiled happily. "Doc kind of figured that one too," he said.

"Put in ten gallons," said Mack. "And don't go leaving none in the hose."

The little expedition did not go through the center of Monterey. A delicacy about the license plates and the lights made Gay choose back streets. There would be the time when they would go up Carmel Hill and down into the Valley, a good four miles on a main highway, exposed to any passing cop until they turned up the fairly unfrequented Carmel Valley road. Gay chose a back street that brought them out on the main highway at Peter's Gate just before the steep Carmel Hill starts. Gay took a good noisy clattering run at the hill and in fifty yards he put the pedal down to low. He knew it wouldn't work, the band was worn too thin. On the level it was all right but not on a hill. He stopped, let the truck back around and aimed it down the hill. Then he gave it the gas and the reverse pedal. And the reverse was not worn. The truck crawled steadily and slowly but backward up Carmel Hill.

And they very nearly made it. The radiator boiled, of course, but most Model T experts believed that it wasn't working well if it wasn't boiling.

Someone should write an erudite essay on the moral, physical, and esthetic effect of the Model T Ford on the American nation. Two generations of Americans knew more about the Ford coil than the clitoris, about the planetary system of gears than the

solar system of stars. With the Model T, part of the
concept of private property disappeared. Pliers ceased
to be privately owned and a tire pump belonged to the
last man who had picked it up. Most of the babies of
the period were conceived in Model T Fords and not a
few were born in them. The theory of the Anglo Saxon
home became so warped that it never quite recovered.

The truck backed sturdily up Carmel Hill and it got
past the Jack's Peak road and was just going into the
last and steepest pull when the motor's breathing
thickened, gulped, and strangled. It seemed very quiet
when the motor was still. Gay, who was heading
downhill anyway, ran down the hill fifty feet and
turned into the Jack's Peak road entrance.

"What is it?" Mack asked.

"Carburetor, I think," said Gay. The engine sizzled
and creaked with heat and the jet of steam that blew
down the overflow pipe sounded like the hiss of an
alligator.

The carburetor of a Model T is not complicated but
it needs all of its parts to function. There is a needle
valve, and the point must be on the needle and must
sit in its hole or the carburetor does not work.

Gay held the needle in his hand and the point was
broken off. "How in hell you s'pose that happened?"
he asked.

"Magic," said Mack, "just pure magic. Can you fix
it?"

"Hell, no," said Gay. "Got to get another one."

"How much they cost?"

"About a buck if you buy one new—quarter at a
wrecker's."

"You got a buck?" Mack asked.

"Yeah, but I won't need it."

"Well, get back as soon as you can, will you? We'll just stay right here."

"Anyways you won't go running off without a needle valve," said Gay. He stepped out to the road. He thumbed three cars before one stopped for him. The boys watched him climb in and start down the hill. They didn't see him again for one hundred and eighty days.

Oh, the infinity of possibility! How could it happen that the car that picked up Gay broke down before it got into Monterey? If Gay had not been a mechanic, he would not have fixed the car. If he had not fixed it the owner wouldn't have taken him to Jimmy Brucia's for a drink. And why was it Jimmy's birthday? Out of all the possibilities in the world—the millions of them—only events occurred that lead to the Salinas jail. Sparky Enea and Tiny Colletti had made up a quarrel and were helping Jimmy to celebrate his birthday. The blonde came in. The musical argument in front of the juke box. Gay's new friend who knew a judo hold and tried to show it to Sparky and got his wrist broken when the hold went wrong. The policeman with a bad stomach—all unrelated, irrelevant details and yet all running in one direction. Fate just didn't intend Gay to go on that frog hunt and Fate took a hell of a lot of trouble and people and accidents to keep him from it. When the final climax came with the front of Holman's bootery broken out and the party trying on the shoes in the display window only Gay didn't hear the fire whistle. Only Gay didn't go to the fire and when the police came they found him sitting all alone in Holman's window wearing one brown oxford and one patent leather dress shoe with a gray cloth top.

Back at the truck the boys built a little fire when it got dark and the chill crept up from the ocean. The pines above them soughed in the fresh sea wind. The boys lay in the pine needles and looked at the lonely sky through the pine branches. For a while they spoke of the difficulties Gay must be having getting a needle valve and then gradually as the time passed they didn't mention him any more.

"Somebody should of gone with him," said Mack.

About ten o'clock Eddie got up. "There's a construction camp a piece up the hill," he said. "I think I'll go up and see if they got any Model T's."

12

Monterey is a city with a long and brilliant literary tradition. It remembers with pleasure and some glory that Robert Louis Stevenson lived there. Treasure Island certainly has the topography and the coastal plan of Pt. Lobos. More recently in Carmel there have been a great number of literary men about, but there is not the old flavor, the old dignity of the true belles-lettres. Once the town was greatly outraged over what the citizens considered a slight to an author. It had to do with the death of Josh Billings, the great humorist.

Where the new postoffice is, there used to be a deep gulch with water flowing in it and a little foot bridge over it. On one side of the gulch was a fine old adobe and on the other the house of the doctor who handled all the sickness, birth, and death in the town. He worked with animals too and, having studied in France, he even dabbled in the new practice of embalming bodies before they were buried. Some of the old-timers considered this sentimental and some thought it wasteful and to some it was sacrilegious since there was no provision for it in any sacred volume. But the better and richer families were coming to it and it looked to become a fad.

One morning elderly Mr. Carriaga was walking from his house on the hill down toward Alvarado Street. He was just crossing the foot bridge when his attention was drawn to a small boy and a dog struggling up out of the gulch. The boy carried a liver while the dog dragged yards of intestine at the end of which a stomach dangled. Mr. Carriaga paused and addressed the little boy politely: "Good morning."

In those days little boys were courteous. "Good morning, sir."

"Where are you going with the liver?"

"I'm going to make some chum and catch some mackerel."

Mr. Carriaga smiled. "And the dog, will he catch mackerel too?"

"The dog found that. It's his, sir. We found them in the gulch."

Mr. Carriaga smiled and strolled on and then his mind began to work. That isn't a beef liver, it's too small. And it isn't a calf's liver, it's too red. It isn't a sheep's liver— Now his mind was alert. At the corner he met Mr. Ryan.

"Anyone die in Monterey last night?" he asked.

"Not that I know of," said Mr. Ryan.

"Anyone killed?"

"No."

They walked on together and Mr. Carriaga told about the little boy and the dog.

At the Adobe Bar a number of citizens were gathered for their morning conversation. There Mr. Carriaga told his story again and he had just finished when the constable came into the Adobe. He should know if anyone had died. "No one died in Monterey," he said. "But Josh Billings died out at the Hotel del Monte."

The men in the bar were silent. And the same thought went through all their minds. Josh Billings was a great man, a great writer. He had honored Monterey by dying there and he had been degraded. Without much discussion a committee formed made up of everyone there. The stern men walked quickly to the gulch and across the foot bridge and they hammered on the door of the doctor who had studied in France.

He had worked late. The knocking got him out of bed and brought him tousled of hair and beard to the door in his nightgown. Mr. Carriaga addressed him sternly: "Did you embalm Josh Billings?"

"Why—yes."

"What did you do with his tripas?"

"Why—I threw them in the gulch where I always do."

They made him dress quickly then and they hurried down to the beach. If the little boy had gone quickly about his business, it would have been too late. He was just getting into a boat when the committee arrived. The intestine was in the sand where the dog had abandoned it.

Then the French doctor was made to collect the parts. He was forced to wash them reverently and pick out as much sand as possible. The doctor himself had to stand the expense of the leaden box which went into the coffin of Josh Billings. For Monterey was not a town to let dishonor come to a literary man.

13

      Mack and the boys slept peacefully on the pine needles. Some time before dawn Eddie came back. He had gone a long way before he found a Model T. And then when he did, he wondered whether or not it would be a good idea to take the needle out of its seat. It might not fit. So he took the whole carburetor. The boys didn't wake up when he got back. He lay down beside them and slept under the pine trees. There was one nice thing about Model T's. The parts were not only interchangeable, they were unidentifiable.

There is a beautiful view from the Carmel grade, the curving bay with the waves creaming on the sand, the dune country around Seaside and right at the bottom of the hill, the warm intimacy of the town.

Mack got up in the dawn and hustled his pants where they bound him and he stood looking down on the bay. He could see some of the purse-seiners coming in. A tanker stood over against Seaside, taking on oil. Behind him the rabbits stirred in the bush. Then the sun came up and shook the night chill out of the

air the way you'd shake a rug. When he felt the first
sun warmth, Mack shivered.

The boys ate a little bread while Eddie installed the
new carburetor. And when it was ready, they didn't
bother to crank it. They pushed it out to the highway
and coasted in gear until it started. And then Eddie
driving, they backed up over the rise, over the top and
turned and headed forward and down past Hatton
Fields. In Carmel Valley the artichoke plants stood
gray green, and the willows were lush along the river.
They turned left up the valley. Luck blossomed from
the first. A dusty Rhode Island red rooster who had
wandered too far from his own farmyard crossed the
road and Eddie hit him without running too far off the
road. Sitting in the back of the truck, Hazel picked
him as they went and let the feathers fly from his
hand, the most widely distributed evidence on record,
for there was a little breeze in the morning blowing
down from Jamesburg and some of the red chicken
feathers were deposited on Pt. Lobos and some even
blew out to sea.

The Carmel is a lovely little river. It isn't very long
but in its course it has everything a river should have.
It rises in the mountains, and tumbles down a while,
runs through shallows, is dammed to make a lake,
spills over the dam, crackles among round boulders,
wanders lazily under sycamores, spills into pools
where trout live, drops in against banks where crayfish
live. In the winter it becomes a torrent, a mean little
fierce river, and in the summer it is a place for children to wade in and for fishermen to wander in. Frogs
blink from its banks and the deep ferns grow beside it.
Deer and foxes come to drink from it, secretly in the

morning and evening, and now and then a mountain lion crouched flat laps its water. The farms of the rich little valley back up to the river and take its water for the orchards and the vegetables. The quail call beside it and the wild doves come whistling in at dusk. Raccoons pace its edges looking for frogs. It's everything a river should be.

A few miles up the valley the river cuts in under a high cliff from which vines and ferns hang down. At the base of this cliff there is a pool, green and deep, and on the other side of the pool there is a little sandy place where it is good to sit and to cook your dinner.

Mack and the boys came down to this place happily. It was perfect. If frogs were available, they would be here. It was a place to relax, a place to be happy. On the way out they had thriven. In addition to the big red chicken there was a sack of carrots which had fallen from a vegetable truck, half a dozen onions which had not. Mack had a bag of coffee in his pocket. In the truck there was a five-gallon can with the top cut off. The wining jug was nearly half full. Such things as salt and pepper had been brought. Mack and the boys would have thought anyone who traveled without salt, pepper, and coffee very silly indeed.

Without effort, confusion, or much thought, four round stones were rolled together on the little beach. The rooster who had challenged the sunrise of this very day lay dismembered and clean in water in the five-gallon can with peeled onions about him, while a little fire of dead willow sticks sputtered between the stones, a very little fire. Only fools build big fires. It would take a long time to cook this rooster, for it had taken him a long time to achieve his size and muscularity. But as the water began to boil gently about him, he smelled good from the beginning.

Mack gave them a pep talk. "The best time for frogs is at night," he said, "so I guess we'll just lay around 'til it gets dark." They sat in the shade and gradually one by one they stretched out and slept.

Mack was right. Frogs do not move around much in the daytime; they hide under ferns and they look secretly out of holes under rocks. The way to catch frogs is with a flashlight at night. The men slept knowing they might have a very active night. Only Hazel stayed awake to replenish the little fire under the cooking chicken.

There is no golden afternoon next to the cliff. When the sun went over it at about two o'clock a whispering shade came to the beach. The sycamores rustled in the afternoon breeze. Little water snakes slipped down to the rocks and then gently entered the water and swam along through the pool, their heads held up like little periscopes and a tiny wake spreading behind them. A big trout jumped in the pool. The gnats and mosquitoes which avoid the sun came out and buzzed over the water. All of the sun bugs, the flies, the dragonflies, the wasps, the hornets, went home. And as the shadow came to the beach, as the first quail began to call, Mack and the boys awakened. The smell of the chicken stew was heartbreaking. Hazel had picked a fresh bay leaf from a tree by the river and he had dropped it in. The carrots were in now. Coffee in its own can was simmering on its own rock, far enough from the flame so that it did not boil too hard. Mack awakened, started up, stretched, staggered to the pool, washed his face with cupped hands, hacked, spat, washed out his mouth, broke wind, tightened his belt, scratched his legs, combed his wet hair with his fingers, drank from the jug, belched and sat down by the fire. "By God that smells good," he said.

Men all do about the same things when they wake up. Mack's process was loosely the one all of them followed. And soon they had all come to the fire and complimented Hazel. Hazel stuck his pocket knife into the muscles of the chicken.

"He ain't going to be what you'd call tender," said Hazel. "You'd have to cook him about two weeks to get him tender. How old about do you judge he was, Mack?"

"I'm forty-eight and I ain't as tough as he is," said Mack.

Eddie said, "How old can a chicken get, do you think—that's if nobody pushes him around or he don't get sick?"

"That's something nobody isn't ever going to find out," said Jones.

It was a pleasant time. The jug went around and warmed them.

Jones said, "Eddie, I don't mean to complain none. I was just thinkin'. S'pose you had two or three jugs back of the bar. S'pose you put all the whiskey in one and all the wine in another and all the beer in another—"

A slightly shocked silence followed the suggestion. "I didn't mean nothing," said Jones quickly. "I like it this way—" Jones talked too much then because he knew he had made a social blunder and he wasn't able to stop. "What I like about it this way is you never know what kind of a drunk you're going to get out of it," he said. "You take whiskey," he said hurriedly. "You more or less knows what you'll do. A fightin' guy fights and a cryin' guy cries, but this—" he said magnanimously—"why you don't know whether it'll run you up a pine tree or start you swimming to Santa Cruz. It's more fun that way," he said weakly.

"Speaking of swimming," said Mack to fill in the indelicate place in the conversation and to shut Jones up. "I wonder whatever happened to that guy McKinley Moran. Remember that deep sea diver?"

"I remember him," said Hughie. "I and him used to hang around together. He just didn't get much work and then he got to drinking. It's kind of tough on you divin' and drinkin'. Got to worryin' too. Finally he sold his suit and helmet and pump and went on a hell of a drunk and then he left town. I don't know where he went. He wasn't no good after he went down after that Wop that got took down with the anchor from the Twelve Brothers. McKinley just dove down. Bust his eardrums, and he wasn't no good after that. Didn't hurt the Wop a bit."

Mack sampled the jug again. "He used to make a lot of dough during Prohibition," Mack said. "Used to get twenty-five bucks a day from the government to dive lookin' for liquor on the bottom and he got three dollars a case from Louie for not findin' it. Had it worked out so he brought up one case a day to keep the government happy. Louie didn't mind that none. Made it so they didn't get in no new divers. McKinley made a lot of dough."

"Yeah," said Hughie. "But he's like everybody else—gets some dough and he wants to get married. He got married three times before his dough run out. I

could always tell. He'd buy a white fox fur piece and
bang!—next thing you'd know, he's married."

"I wonder what happened to Gay," Eddie asked. It
was the first time they had spoken of him.

"Same thing, I guess," said Mack. "You just can't
trust a married guy. No matter how much he hates his
old lady why he'll go back to her. Get to thinkin' and
broodin' and back he'll go. You can't trust him no
more. Take Gay," said Mack. "His old lady hits him.
But I bet you when Gay's away from her three days, he
gets it figured out that it's his fault and he goes back to
make it up to her."

They ate long and daintily, spearing out pieces of
chicken, holding the dripping pieces until they cooled
and then gnawing the muscled meat from the bone.
They speared the carrots on pointed willow switches
and finally they passed the can and drank the juice.
And around them the evening crept in as delicately as
music. The quail called each other down to the water.
The trout jumped in the pool. And the moths came
down and fluttered about the pool as the daylight
mixed into the darkness. They passed the coffee can
about and they were warm and fed and silent. At last
Mack said, "God damn it. I hate a liar."

"Who's been lyin' to you?" Eddie asked.

"Oh, I don't mind a guy that tells a little one to get
along or to hop up a conversation, but I hate a guy that
lies to himself."

"Who done that?" Eddie asked.

"Me," said Mack. "And maybe you guys. Here we
are," he said earnestly, "the whole God damned
shabby lot of us. We worked it out that we wanted to
give Doc a party. So we come out here and have a hell

of a lot of fun. Then we'll go back and get the dough from Doc. There's five of us, so we'll drink five times as much liquor as he will. And I ain't sure we're doin' it for Doc. I ain't sure we ain't doin' it for ourselves. And Doc's too nice a fella to do that to. Doc is the nicest fella I ever knew. I don't want to be the kind of guy that would take advantage of him. You know one time I put the bee on him for a buck. I give him a hell of a story. Right in the middle I seen he knew God damn well the story was so much malarky. So right in the middle I says, 'Doc, that's a fuggin' lie!' And he put his hand in his pocket and brought out a buck. 'Mack,' he says, 'I figure a guy that needs it bad enough to make up a lie to get it, really needs it,' and he give me the buck. I paid him that buck back the next day. I never did spend it. Just kept it overnight and then give it back to him."

Hazel said, "There ain't nobody likes a party better than Doc. We're givin' him the party. What the hell is the beef?"

"I don't know," said Mack, "I'd just like to give him something when I didn't get most of it back."

"How about a present?" Hughie suggested. "S'pose we just bought the whiskey and give it to him and let him do what he wants."

"Now you're talkin'," said Mack. "That's just what we'll do. We'll just give him the whiskey and fade out."

"You know what'll happen," said Eddie. "Henri and them people from Carmel will smell that whiskey out and then instead of only five of us there'll be twenty. Doc told me one time himself they can smell him fryin' a steak from Cannery Row clear down to Point Sur. I don't see the percentage. He'd come out better if we give him the party ourselves."

Mack considered this reasoning. "Maybe you're right," he said at last. "But s'pose we give him something except whiskey, maybe cuff links with his initials."

"Oh, horse shit," said Hazel. "Doc don't want stuff like that."

The night was in by now and the stars were white in the sky. Hazel fed the fire and it put a little room of light on the beach. Over the hill a fox was barking sharply. And now in the night the smell of sage came down from the hills. The water chuckled on the stones where it went out of the deep pool.

Mack was mulling over the last piece of reasoning when the sound of footsteps on the ground made them turn. A man dark and large stalked near and he had a shotgun over his arm and a pointer walked shyly and delicately at his heel.

"What the hell are you doing here?" he asked.

"Nothing," said Mack.

"The land's posted. No fishing, hunting, fires, camping. Now you just pack up and put that fire out and get off this land."

Mack stood up humbly. "I didn't know, Captain," he said. "Honest we never seen the sign, Captain."

"There's signs all over. You couldn't have missed them."

"Look, Captain, we made a mistake and we're sorry," said Mack. He paused and looked closely at the slouching figure. "You are a military man, aren't you, sir? I can always tell. Military man don't carry his shoulders the same as ordinary people. I was in the army so long, I can always tell."

Imperceptibly the shoulders of the man straightened, nothing obvious, but he held himself differently.

"I don't allow fires on my place," he said.

"Well, we're sorry," said Mack. "We'll get right out, Captain. You see, we're workin' for some scientists. We're tryin' to get some frogs. They're workin' on cancer and we're helpin' out getting some frogs."

The man hesitated for a moment. "What do they do with the frogs?" he asked.

"Well, sir," said Mack, "they give cancer to the frogs and then they can study and experiment and they got it nearly licked if they can just get some frogs. But if you don't want us on your land, Captain, we'll get right out. Never would of come in if we knew." Suddenly Mack seemed to see the pointer for the first time. "By God that's a fine-lookin' bitch," he said enthusiastically. "She looks like Nola that win the field trials in Virginia last year. She a Virginia dog, Captain?"

The captain hesitated and then he lied. "Yes," he said shortly. "She's lame. Tick got her right on her shoulder."

Mack was instantly solicitous. "Mind if I look, Captain? Come, girl. Come on, girl." The pointer looked up at her master and then sidled up to Mack. "Pile on some twigs so I can see," he said to Hazel.

"It's up where she can't lick it," said the captain and he leaned over Mack's shoulder to look.

Mack pressed some pus out of the evil-looking crater on the dog's shoulder. "I had a dog once had a thing like this and it went right in and killed him. She just had pups, didn't she?"

"Yes," said the captain, "six. I put iodine on that place."

"No," said Mack, "that won't draw. You got any epsom salts up at your place?"

"Yes—there's a big bottle."

"Well you make a hot poultice of epsom salts and put it on there. She's weak, you know, from the pups. Be a shame if she got sick now. You'd lose the pups too." The pointer looked deep into Mack's eyes and then she licked his hand.

"Tell you what I'll do, Captain. I'll look after her myself. Epsom salt'll do the trick. That's the best thing."

The captain stroked the dog's head. "You know, I've got a pond up by the house that's so full of frogs I can't sleep nights. Why don't you look up there? They bellow all night. I'd be glad to get rid of them."

"That's mighty nice of you," said Mack. "I'll bet those docs would thank you for that. But I'd like to get a poultice on this dog." He turned to the others. "You put out this fire," he said. "Make sure there ain't a spark left and clean up around. You don't want to leave no mess. I and the captain will go and take care of Nola here. You fellows follow along when you get cleared up." Mack and the captain walked away together.

Hazel kicked sand on the fire. "I bet Mack could of been president of the U.S. if he wanted," he said.

"What could he do with it if he had it?" Jones asked. "There wouldn't be no fun in that."

14

Early morning is a time of magic in Cannery Row. In the gray time after the light has come and before the sun has risen, the Row seems to hang suspended out of time in a silvery light. The street lights go out, and the weeds are a brilliant green. The corrugated iron of the canneries glows with the pearly lucence of platinum or old pewter. No automobiles are running then. The street is silent of progress and business. And the rush and drag of the waves can be heard as they splash in among the piles of the canneries. It is a time of great peace, a deserted time, a little era of rest. Cats drip over the fences and slither like syrup over the ground to look for fish heads. Silent early morning dogs parade majestically picking and choosing judiciously whereon to pee. The sea gulls come flapping in to sit on the cannery roofs to await the day of refuse. They sit on the roof peaks shoulder to shoulder. From the rocks near the Hopkins Marine Station comes the barking of sea lions like the baying of hounds. The air is cool and fresh. In the back gardens the gophers push up the morning mounds of fresh damp earth and they creep out and drag flowers into their holes. Very few people are about, just enough to make it seem more deserted than it is. One of Dora's girls comes home from a call on a patron too wealthy or too sick to visit the Bear Flag. Her makeup is a little sticky and her feet are tired. Lee Chong brings the garbage cans out and stands them on the curb. The old Chinaman comes out of the sea and flap-flaps across the street and up past the Palace. The cannery watchmen look out and blink at the morning light. The bouncer at the Bear Flag steps out on the porch in his shirtsleeves and stretches and yawns and scratches his stomach. The snores of Mr. Malloy's tenants in the pipes have a deep tunnelly quality. It is the hour of the pearl—the interval between day and night when time stops and examines itself.

On such a morning and in such a light two soldiers and two girls strolled easily along the street. They had come out of La Ida and they were very tired and very happy. The girls were hefty, big breasted and strong and their blonde hair was in slight disarray. They wore printed rayon party dresses, wrinkled now and clinging to their convexities. And each girl wore a soldier's cap, one far back on her head and the other with the visor down almost on her nose. They were full-lipped, broad-nosed, hippy girls and they were very tired.

The soldiers' tunics were unbuttoned and their belts were threaded through their epaulets. The ties were pulled down a little so the shirt collars could be unbuttoned. And the soldiers wore the girls' hats, one a tiny yellow straw boater with a bunch of daisies on the crown, the other a white knitted half-hat to which medallions of blue cellophane adhered. They walked

holding hands, swinging their hands rhythmically. The
soldier on the outside had a large brown paper bag
filled with cold canned beer. They strolled softly in the
pearly light. They had had a hell of a time and they
felt good. They smiled delicately like weary children
remembering a party. They looked at one another and
smiled and they swung their hands. Past the Bear Flag
they went and said "Hiya," to the bouncer who was
scratching his stomach. They listened to the snores
from the pipes and laughed a little. At Lee Chong's
they stopped and looked into the messy display window where tools and clothes and food crowded for
attention. Swinging their hands and scuffling their
feet, they came to the end of Cannery Row and turned
up to the railroad track. The girls climbed up on the
rails and walked along on them and the soldiers put
their arms around the plump waists to keep them from
falling. Then they went past the boat works and turned
down into the park-like property of the Hopkins Marine Station. There is a tiny curved beach in front of
the station, a miniature beach between little reefs. The
gentle morning waves licked up the beach and whis-
pered softly. The fine smell of seaweed came from the
exposed rocks. As the four came to the beach a sliver
of the sun broke over Tom Work's land across the head
of the bay and it gilded the water and made the rocks
yellow. The girls sat formally down in the sand and
straightened their skirts over their knees. One of the
soldiers punched holes in four cans of beer and
handed them around. And then the men lay down and
put their heads in the girls' laps and looked up into
their faces. And they smiled at each other, a tired and
peaceful and wonderful secret.

From up near the station came the barking of a
dog—the watchman, a dark and surly man, had seen
them and his black and surly cocker spaniel had seen
them. He shouted at them and when they did not move
he came down on the beach and his dog barked monotonously. "Don't you know you can't lay around
here? You got to get off. This is private property!"

The soldiers did not even seem to hear him. They
smiled on and the girls were stroking their hair over
the temples. At last in slow motion one of the soldiers
turned his head so that his cheek was cradled between
the girl's legs. He smiled benevolently at the caretaker. "Why don't you take a flying fuggut the moon?"
he said kindly and he turned back to look at the girl.

The sun lighted her blonde hair and she scratched
him over one ear. They didn't even see the caretaker
go back to his house.

15

By the time the boys got up to the farmhouse Mack was in the kitchen. The pointer bitch lay on her side, and Mack held a cloth saturated with epsom salts against her tick bite. Among her legs the big fat wiener pups nuzzled and bumped for milk and the bitch looked patiently up into Mack's face saying, "You see how it is? I try to tell him but he doesn't understand."

The captain held a lamp and looked down on Mack. "I'm glad to know about that," he said.

Mack said, "I don't want to tell you about your business, sir, but these pups ought to be weaned. She ain't got a hell of a lot of milk left and them pups are chewin' her to pieces."

"I know," said the captain. "I s'pose I should have drowned them all but one. I've been so busy trying to keep the place going. People don't take the interest in bird dogs they used to. It's all poodles and boxers and Dobermans."

"I know," said Mack. "And there ain't no dog like a pointer for a man. I don't know what's come over people. But you wouldn't of drowned them, would you, sir?"

"Well," said the captain, "since my wife went into politics, I'm just running crazy. She got elected to the Assembly for this district and when the Legislature isn't in session, she's off making speeches. And when she's home she's studying all the time and writing bills."

"Must be lousy in—I mean it must be pretty lonely," said Mack. "Now if I had a pup like this—" he picked up a squirming fuzz-faced pup—"why I bet I'd have a real bird dog in three years. I'd take a bitch every time."

"Would you like to have one?" the captain asked.

Mack looked up. "You mean you'd let me have one? Oh! Jesus Christ yes."

"Take your pick," said the captain. "Nobody seems to understand bird dogs any more."

The boys stood in the kitchen and gathered quick impressions. It was obvious that the wife was away— the opened cans, the frying pan with lace from fried eggs still sticking to it, the crumbs on the kitchen table, the open box of shotgun shells on the bread box all shrieked of the lack of a woman, while the white curtains and the papers on the dish shelves and the too small towels on the rack told them a woman had been there. And they were unconsciously glad she wasn't there. The kind of women who put papers on shelves and had little towels like that instinctively distrusted and disliked Mack and the boys. Such women knew that they were the worst threats to a home, for they offered ease and thought and companionship as opposed to neatness, order, and properness. They were very glad she was away.

Now the captain seemed to feel that they were doing him a favor. He didn't want them to leave. He said hesitantly, "S'pose you boys would like a little something to warm you up before you go out for the frogs?"

The others looked at Mack. Mack was frowning as though he was thinking it through. "When we're out doin' scientific stuff, we make it a kind of rule not to touch nothin'," he said, and then quickly as though he might have gone too far, "But seein' as how you been so nice to us—well I wouldn't mind a short one myself. I don't know about the boys."

The boys agreed that they wouldn't mind a short one either. The captain got a flashlight and went down in the cellar. They could hear him moving lumber and boxes about and he came back upstairs with a five-gallon oak keg in his arms. He set it on the table. "During Prohibition I got some corn whiskey and laid it away. I just got to thinking I'd like to see how it is. It's pretty old now. I'd almost forgot it. You see—my wife—" he let it go at that because it was apparent that they understood. The captain knocked out the oak plug from the end of the keg and got glasses down from the shelf that had scallop-edged paper laid on it. It is a hard job to pour a small drink from a five-gallon keg. Each of them got half a water glass of the clear brown liquor. They waited ceremoniously for the captain and then they said, "Over the river," and tossed it back. They swallowed, tasted their tongues, sucked their lips, and there was a far-away look in their eyes.

Mack peered into his empty glass as though some holy message were written in the bottom. And then he raised his eyes. "You can't say nothin' about that," he

said. "They don't put that in bottles." He breathed in
deeply and sucked his breath as it came out. "I don't
think I ever tasted nothin' as good as that," he said.

The captain looked pleased. His glance wandered
back to the keg. "It is good," he said. "You think we
might have another little one?"

Mack stared into his glass again. "Maybe a short
one," he agreed. "Wouldn't it be easier to pour out
some in a pitcher? You're liable to spill it that way."

Two hours later they recalled what they had come
for.

The frog pool was square—fifty feet wide and seventy feet long and four feet deep. Lush soft grass grew
about its edge and a little ditch brought the water from
the river to it and from it little ditches went out to the
orchards. There were frogs there all right, thousands of
them. Their voices beat the night, they boomed and
barked and croaked and rattled. They sang to the
stars, to the waning moon, to the waving grasses. They
bellowed love songs and challenges. The men crept
through the darkness toward the pool. The captain
carried a nearly filled pitcher of whiskey and every
man had his own glass. The captain had found them
flashlights that worked. Hughie and Jones carried
gunny sacks. As they drew quietly near, the frogs
heard them coming. The night had been roaring with
frog song and then suddenly it was silent. Mack and
the boys and the captain sat down on the ground to
have one last short one and to map their campaign.
And the plan was bold.

During the millennia that frogs and men have lived
in the same world, it is probable that men have hunted

frogs. And during that time a pattern of hunt and parry
has developed. The man with net or bow or lance or
gun creeps noiselessly, as he thinks, toward the frog.
The pattern requires that the frog sit still, sit very still
and wait. The rules of the game require the frog to wait
until the final flicker of a second, when the net is
descending, when the lance is in the air, when the
finger squeezes the trigger, then the frog jumps, plops
into the water, swims to the bottom and waits until the
man goes away. That is the way it is done, the way it
has always been done. Frogs have every right to expect
it will always be done that way. Now and then the net
is too quick, the lance pierces, the gun flicks and that
frog is gone, but it is all fair and in the framework.
Frogs don't resent that. But how could they have an-
ticipated Mack's new method? How could they have
foreseen the horror that followed? The sudden flashing
of lights, the shouting and squealing of men, the rush
of feet. Every frog leaped, plopped into the pool, and
swam frantically to the bottom. Then into the pool
plunged the line of men, stamping, churning, moving
in a crazy line up the pool, flinging their feet about.
Hysterically the frogs displaced from their placid spots
swam ahead of the crazy thrashing feet and the feet
came on. Frogs are good swimmers but they haven't
much endurance. Down the pool they went until finally
they were bunched and crowded against the end. And
the feet and wildly plunging bodies followed them. A
few frogs lost their heads and floundered among the
feet and got through and these were saved. But the
majority decided to leave this pool forever, to find a
new home in a new country where this kind of thing

didn't happen. A wave of frantic, frustrated frogs, big ones, little ones, brown ones, green ones, men frogs and women frogs, a wave of them broke over the bank, crawled, leaped, scrambled. They clambered up the grass, they clutched at each other, little ones rode on big ones. And then—horror on horror—the flashlights found them. Two men gathered them like berries. The line came out of the water and closed in on their rear and gathered them like potatoes. Tens and fifties of them were flung into the gunny sacks, and the sacks filled with tired, frightened, and disillusioned frogs, with dripping, whimpering frogs. Some got away, of course, and some had been saved in the pool. But never in frog history had such an execution taken place. Frogs by the pound, by the fifty pounds. They weren't counted but there must have been six or seven hundred. Then happily Mack tied up the necks of the sacks. They were soaking, dripping wet and the air was cool. They had a short one in the grass before they went back to the house so they wouldn't catch cold.

It is doubtful whether the captain had ever had so much fun. He was indebted to Mack and the boys. Later when the curtains caught fire and were put out with the little towels, the captain told the boys not to mind it. He felt it was an honor to have them burn his house clear down, if they wanted to. "My wife is a wonderful woman," he said in a kind of peroration. "Most wonderful woman. Ought to of been a man. If she was a man I wouldn' of married her." He laughed a long time over that and repeated it three or four times and resolved to remember it so he could tell it to a lot of other people. He filled a jug with whiskey and gave it to Mack. He wanted to go to live with them in the Palace Flophouse. He decided that his wife would like Mack and the boys if she only knew them. Finally he went to sleep on the floor with his head among the puppies. Mack and the boys poured themselves a short one and regarded him seriously.

Mack said, "He give me that jug of whiskey, didn't he? You heard him?"

"Sure he did," said Eddie. "I heard him."

"And he give me a pup?"

"Sure, pick of the litter. We all heard him. Why?"

"I never did roll a drunk and I ain't gonna start now," said Mack. "We got to get out of here. He's gonna wake up feelin' lousy and it's goin' to be all our fault. I just don't want to be here." Mack glanced at the burned curtains, at the floor glistening with whiskey and puppy dirt, at the bacon grease that was co-agulating on the stove front. He went to the pups, looked them over carefully, felt bone and frame, looked in eyes and regarded jaws, and he picked out a beautifully spotted bitch with a liver-colored nose and a fine dark yellow eye. "Come on, darling," he said.

They blew out the lamp because of the danger of fire. It was just turning dawn as they left the house.

"I don't think I ever had such a fine trip," said Mack. "But I got to thinkin' about his wife comin' back and it gave me the shivers." The pup whined in his arms and he put it under his coat. "He's a real nice fella," said Mack. "After you get him feelin' easy, that is." He strode on toward the place where they had parked the Ford. "We shouldn't go forgettin' we're doin' all this for Doc," he said. "From the way things are pannin' out, it looks like Doc is a pretty lucky guy."

16

Probably the busiest time the girls of the Bear Flag ever had was the March of the big sardine catch. It wasn't only that the fish ran in silvery billions and money ran almost as freely. A new regiment moved into the Presidio and a new bunch of soldiers always shop around a good deal before they settle down. Dora was short handed just at that time too, for Eva Flanegan had gone to East St. Louis on a vacation, Phyllis Mae had broken her leg getting out of the roller coaster in Santa Cruz, and Elsie Doublebottom had made a novena and wasn't much good for anything else. The men from the sardine fleet, loaded with dough, were in and out all afternoon. They sail at dark and fish all night so they must play in the afternoon. In the evening the soldiers of the new regiment came down and stood around playing the juke box and drinking Coca-Cola and sizing up the girls for the time when they would be paid. Dora was having trouble with her income tax, for she was entangled in that curious enigma which said the business was illegal and then taxed her for it. In addition to everything else

there were the regulars—the steady customers who
had been coming down for years, the laborers from the
gravel pits, the riders from the ranches, the railroad
men who came in the front door, and the city officials
and prominent business men who came in the rear
entrance back by the tracks and who had little chintz
sitting rooms assigned to them.

All in all it was a terrific month and right in the
middle of it the influenza epidemic had to break out. It
came to the whole town. Mrs. Talbot and her daughter
of the San Carlos Hotel had it. Tom Work had it.
Benjamin Peabody and his wife had it. Excelentísima
Maria Antonia Field had it. The whole Gross family
came down with it.

The doctors of Monterey—and there were enough of
them to take care of the ordinary diseases, accidents
and neuroses—were running crazy. They had more
business than they could do among clients who if they
didn't pay their bills, at least had the money to pay
them. Cannery Row which produces a tougher breed
than the rest of the town was late in contracting it, but
finally it got them too. The schools were closed. There
wasn't a house that hadn't feverish children and sick
parents. It was not a deadly disease as it was in 1917
but with children it had a tendency to go into the
mastoids. The medical profession was very busy, and
besides, Cannery Row was not considered a very good
financial risk.

Now Doc of the Western Biological Laboratory had
no right to practice medicine. It was not his fault that
everyone in the Row came to him for medical advice.
Before he knew it he found himself running from
shanty to shanty taking temperatures, giving physics,

borrowing and delivering blankets and even taking
food from house to house where mothers looked at him
with inflamed eyes from their beds, and thanked him
and put the full responsibility for their children's re-
covery on him. When a case got really out of hand he
phoned a local doctor and sometimes one came if it
seemed to be an emergency. But to the families it was
all emergency. Doc didn't get much sleep. He lived on
beer and canned sardines. In Lee Chong's where he
went to get beer he met Dora who was there to buy a
pair of nail clippers.

"You look done in," Dora said.

"I am," Doc admitted. "I haven't had any sleep for
about a week."

"I know," said Dora. "I hear it's bad. Comes at a
bad time too."

"Well, we haven't lost anybody yet," said Doc. "But
there are some awful sick kids. The Ransel kids have
all developed mastoiditis."

"Is there anything I can do?" Dora asked.

Doc said, "You know there is. People get so scared
and helpless. Take the Ransels—they're scared to
death and they're scared to be alone. If you, or some
of the girls, could just sit with them."

Dora, who was soft as a mouse's belly, could be as
hard as carborundum. She went back to the Bear Flag
and organized it for service. It was a bad time for her
but she did it. The Greek cook made a ten-gallon
cauldron of strong soup and kept it full and kept it
strong. The girls tried to keep up their business but
they went in shifts to sit with the families, and they
carried pots of soup when they went. Doc was in almost constant demand. Dora consulted him and de-

tailed the girls where he suggested. And all the time the business at the Bear Flag was booming. The juke box never stopped playing. The men of the fishing fleet and the soldiers stood in line. And the girls did their work and then they took their pots of soup and went to sit with the Ransels, with the McCarthys, with the Ferrias. The girls slipped out the back door, and sometimes staying with the sleeping children the girls dropped to sleep in their chairs. They didn't use makeup for work any more. They didn't have to. Dora herself said she could have used the total membership of the old ladies' home. It was the busiest time the girls at the Bear Flag could remember. Everyone was glad when it was over.

17

In spite of his friendliness and his friends Doc was a lonely and a set-apart man. Mack probably noticed it more than anybody. In a group, Doc seemed always alone. When the lights were on and the curtains drawn, and the Gregorian music played on the great phonograph, Mack used to look down on the laboratory from the Palace Flophouse. He knew Doc had a girl in there, but Mack used to get a dreadful feeling of loneliness out of it. Even in the dear close contact with a girl Mack felt that Doc would be lonely. Doc was a night crawler. The lights were on in the lab all night and yet he seemed to be up in the daytime too. And the great shrouds of music came out of the lab at any time of the day or night. Sometimes when it was all dark and when it seemed that sleep had come at last, the diamond-true child voices of the Sistine Choir would come from the windows of the laboratory.

Doc had to keep up his collecting. He tried to get to the good tides along the coast. The sea rocks and the beaches were his stock pile. He knew where every-

thing was when he wanted it. All the articles of his
trade were filed away on the coast, sea cradles here,
octopi here, tube worms in another place, sea pansies
in another. He knew where to get them but he could
not go for them exactly when he wanted. For Nature
locked up the items and only released them occasionally. Doc had to know not only the tides but when a
particular low tide was good in a particular place.
When such a low tide occurred, he packed his collecting tools in his car, he packed his jars, his bottles, his
plates and preservatives and he went to the beach or
reef or rock ledge where the animals he needed were
stored.

Now he had an order for small octopi and the near-
est place to get them was the boulder-strewn inter-tidal
zone at La Jolla between Los Angeles and San Diego.
It meant a five-hundred-mile drive each way and his
arrival had to coincide with the retreating waters.

The little octopi live among the boulders imbedded
in sand. Being timid and young, they prefer a bottom
on which there are many caves and little crevices and
lumps of mud where they may hide from predators and
protect themselves from the waves. But on the same
flat there are millions of sea cradles. While filling a
definite order for octopi, Doc could replenish his stock
of the cradles.

Low tide was 5:17 A.M. on a Thursday. If Doc left
Monterey on Wednesday morning he could be there
easily in time for the tide on Thursday. He would have
taken someone with him for company but quite by
accident everyone was away or was busy. Mack and
the boys were up Carmel Valley collecting frogs. Three
young women he knew and would have enjoyed as

companions had jobs and couldn't get away in the
middle of the week. Henri the painter was occupied,
for Holman's Department Store had employed not a
flag-pole sitter but a flag-pole skater. On a tall mast on
top of the store he had a little round platform and there
he was on skates going around and around. He had
been there three days and three nights. He was out to
set a new record for being on skates on a platform. The
previous record was 127 hours so he had some time to
go. Henri had taken up his post across the street at
Red Williams' gas station. Henri was fascinated. He
thought of doing a huge abstraction called Substratum
Dream of a Flag-pole Skater. Henri couldn't leave
town while the skater was up there. He protested that
there were philosophic implications in flag-pole skating that no one had touched. Henri sat in a chair,
leaned back against the lattice which concealed the
door of the men's toilet at Red Williams'. He kept his
eye on the eyrie skating platform and obviously he
couldn't go with Doc to La Jolla. Doc had to go alone
because the tide would not wait.

Early in the morning he got his things together.
Personal things went in a small satchel. Another
satchel held instruments and syringes. Having packed,
he combed and trimmed his brown beard, saw that his
pencils were in his shirt pocket and his magnifying
glass attached to his lapel. He packed the trays,
bottles, glass plates, preservatives, rubber boots and a
blanket into the back of his car. He worked through
the pearly time, washed three days' dishes, put the
garbage into the surf. He closed the doors but did not
lock them and by nine o'clock was on his way.

It took Doc longer to go places than other people.

He didn't drive fast and he stopped and ate hamburgers very often. Driving up to Lighthouse Avenue he waved at a dog that looked around and smiled at him. In Monterey before he even started, he felt hungry and stopped at Herman's for a hamburger and beer. While he ate his sandwich and sipped his beer, a bit of conversation came back to him. Blaisedell, the poet, had said to him, "You love beer so much. I'll bet some day you'll go in and order a beer milk shake." It was a simple piece of foolery but it had bothered Doc ever since. He wondered what a beer milk shake would taste like. The idea gagged him but he couldn't let it alone. It cropped up every time he had a glass of beer. Would it curdle the milk? Would you add sugar? It was like a shrimp ice cream. Once the thing got into your head you couldn't forget it. He finished his sandwich and paid Herman. He purposely didn't look at the milk shake machines lined up so shiny against the back wall. If a man ordered a beer milk shake, he thought, he'd better do it in a town where he wasn't known. But then, a man with a beard, ordering a beer milk shake in a town where he wasn't known—they might call the police. A man with a beard was always a little suspect anyway. You couldn't say you wore a beard because you liked a beard. People didn't like you for telling the truth. You had to say you had a scar so you couldn't shave. Once when Doc was at the University of Chicago he had love trouble and he had worked too hard. He thought it would be nice to take a very long walk. He put on a little knapsack and he walked through Indiana and Kentucky and North Carolina and Georgia clear to Florida. He walked among farmers and mountain people, among the swamp people and fishermen. And everywhere people asked him why he was walking through the country.

Because he loved true things, he tried to explain. He said he was nervous and besides he wanted to see the country, smell the ground and look at grass and birds and trees, to savor the country, and there was no other way to do it save on foot. And people didn't like him for telling the truth. They scowled, or shook and tapped their heads, they laughed as though they knew it was a lie and they appreciated a liar. And some, afraid for their daughters or their pigs, told him to move on, to get going, just not to stop near their place if he knew what was good for him.

And so he stopped trying to tell the truth. He said he was doing it on a bet—that he stood to win a hundred dollars. Everyone liked him then and believed him. They asked him in to dinner and gave him a bed and they put lunches up for him and wished him good luck and thought he was a hell of a fine fellow. Doc still loved true things but he knew it was not a general love and it could be a very dangerous mistress.

Doc didn't stop in Salinas for a hamburger. But he stopped in Gonzales, in King City, and in Paso Robles. He had hamburger and beer at Santa Maria—two in Santa Maria because it was a long pull from there to Santa Barbara. In Santa Barbara he had soup, lettuce and string bean salad, pot roast and mashed potatoes, pineapple pie and blue cheese and coffee, and after that he filled the gas tank and went to the toilet. While the service station checked his oil and tires, Doc washed his face and combed his beard and when he came back to the car a number of potential hitchhikers were waiting.

"Going south, Mister?"

Doc traveled on the highways a good deal. He was an old hand. You have to pick your hitchhikers very carefully. It's best to get an experienced one, for he relapses into silence. But the new ones try to pay for their ride by being interesting. Doc had had a leg talked off by some of these. Then after you have made up your mind about the one you want to take, you protect yourself by saying you aren't going far. If your man turns out too much for you, you can drop him. On the other hand, you may be just lucky and get a man very much worth knowing. Doc made a quick survey of the line and chose his company, a thin-faced sales-man-like man in a blue suit. He had deep lines beside his mouth and dark brooding eyes.

He looked at Doc with dislike. "Going south, Mister?"

"Yes," said Doc, "a little way."

"Mind taking me along?"

"Get in!" said Doc.

When they got to Ventura it was pretty soon after the heavy dinner so Doc only stopped for beer. The hitchhiker hadn't spoken once. Doc pulled up at a roadside stand.

"Want some beer?"

"No," said the hitchhiker. "And I don't mind saying I think it's not a very good idea to drive under the influence of alcohol. It's none of my business what you do with your own life but in this case you've got an automobile and that can be a murderous weapon in the hands of a drunken driver."

At the beginning Doc had been slightly startled. "Get out of the car," he said softly.

"What?"

"I'm going to punch you in the nose," said Doc. "If you aren't out of this car before I count ten— One— two—three—"

The man fumbled at the door catch and backed hurriedly out of the car. But once outside he howled, "I'm going to find an officer. I'm going to have you arrested."

Doc opened the box on the dashboard and took out a monkey wrench. His guest saw the gesture and walked hurriedly away.

Doc walked angrily to the counter of the stand.

The waitress, a blonde beauty with just a hint of a goiter, smiled at him. "What'll it be?"

"Beer milk shake," said Doc.

"What?"

Well here it was and what the hell. Might just as well get it over with now as some time later.

The blonde asked, "Are you kidding?"

Doc knew wearily that he couldn't explain, couldn't tell the truth. "I've got a bladder complaint," he said. "Bipalychaetorsonectomy the doctors call it. I'm supposed to drink a *beer milk shake*. Doctor's orders."

The blonde smiled reassuringly. "Oh! I thought you was kidding," she said archly. "You tell me how to make it. I didn't know you was sick."

"Very sick," said Doc, "and due to be sicker. Put in some milk, and add half a bottle of beer. Give me the other half in a glass—no sugar in the milk shake." When she served it, he tasted it wryly. And it wasn't so bad—it just tasted like stale beer and milk.

"It sounds awful," said the blonde.

"It's not so bad when you get used to it," said Doc. "I've been drinking it for seventeen years."

18

Doc had driven slowly. It was late afternoon when he stopped in Ventura, so late in fact that when he stopped in Carpenteria he only had a cheese sandwich and went to the toilet. Besides he intended to get a good dinner in Los Angeles and it was dark when he got there. He drove on through and stopped at a big Chicken-in-the-Rough place he knew about. And there he had fried chicken, julienne potatoes, hot biscuits and honey, and a piece of pineapple pie and blue cheese. And here he filled his thermos bottle with hot coffee, had them make up six ham sandwiches and bought two quarts of beer for breakfast.

It was not so interesting driving at night. No dogs to see, only the highway lighted with his headlights. Doc speeded up to finish the trip. It was about two o'clock when he got to La Jolla. He drove through the town and down to the cliff below which his tidal flat lay. There he stopped the car, ate a sandwich, drank some beer, turned out the lights and curled up in the seat to sleep.

He didn't need a clock. He had been working in a

tidal pattern so long that he could feel a tide change in his sleep. In the dawn he awakened, looked out through the windshield and saw that the water was already retreating down the bouldery flat. He drank some hot coffee, ate three sandwiches and had a quart of beer.

The tide goes out imperceptibly. The boulders show and seem to rise up and the ocean recedes leaving little pools, leaving wet weed and moss and sponge, iridescence and brown and blue and China red. On the bottoms lie the incredible refuse of the sea, shells broken and chipped and bits of skeleton, claws, the whole sea bottom a fantastic cemetery on which the living scamper and scramble.

Doc pulled on his rubber boots and set his rain hat fussily. He took his buckets and jars and his crowbar and put his sandwiches in one pocket and his thermos bottle in another pocket and he went down the cliff to the tidal flat. Then he worked down the flat after the retreating sea. He turned over the boulders with his crowbar and now and then his hand darted quickly into the standing water and brought out a little angry squirming octopus which blushed with rage and spat ink on his hand. Then he dropped it into a jar of sea water with the others and usually the newcomer was so angry that it attacked its fellows.

It was good hunting that day. He got twenty-two little octopi. And he picked off several hundred sea cradles and put them in his wooden bucket. As the tide moved out he followed it while the morning came and the sun arose. The flat extended out two hundred yards and then there was a line of heavy weed-crusted rocks before it dropped off to deep water. Doc worked

out to the barrier edge. He had about what he wanted
now and the rest of the time he looked under stones,
leaned down and peered into the tide pools with their
brilliant mosaics and their scuttling, bubbling life.
And he came at last to the outer barrier where the long
leathery brown algae hung down into the water. Red
starfish clustered on the rocks and the sea pulsed up
and down against the barrier waiting to get in again.
Between two weeded rocks on the barrier Doc saw a
flash of white under water and then the floating weed
covered it. He climbed to the place over the slippery
rocks, held himself firmly, and gently reached down
and parted the brown algae. Then he grew rigid. A
girl's face looked up at him, a pretty, pale girl with
dark hair. The eyes were open and clear and the face
was firm and the hair washed gently about her head.
The body was out of sight, caught in the crevice. The
lips were slightly parted and the teeth showed and on
the face was only comfort and rest. Just under water it
was and the clear water made it very beautiful. It
seemed to Doc that he looked at it for many minutes,
and the face burned into his picture memory.

Very slowly he raised his hand and let the brown
weed float back and cover the face. Doc's heart
pounded deeply and his throat felt tight. He picked up
his bucket and his jars and his crowbar and went
slowly over the slippery rocks back toward the beach.

And the girl's face went ahead of him. He sat down
on the beach in the coarse dry sand and pulled off his
boots. In the jar the little octopi were huddled up,
each keeping as far as possible from the others. Music
sounded in Doc's ears, a high thin piercingly sweet
flute carrying a melody he could never remember, and

against this, a pounding surf-like wood-wind section. The flute went up into regions beyond the hearing range and even there it carried its unbelievable melody. Goose pimples came out on Doc's arms. He shivered and his eyes were wet the way they get in the focus of great beauty. The girl's eyes had been gray and clear and the dark hair floated, drifted lightly over the face. The picture was set for all time. He sat there while the first little spout of water came over the reef bringing the returning tide. He sat there hearing the music while the sea crept in again over the bouldery flat. His hand tapped out the rhythm, and the terrifying flute played in his brain. The eyes were gray and the mouth smiled a little or seemed to catch its breath in ecstasy.

A voice seemed to awaken him. A man stood over him. "Been fishing?"

"No, collecting."

"Well—what are them things?"

"Baby octopi."

"You mean devilfish? I didn't know there was any there. I've lived here all my life."

"You've got to look for them," said Doc listlessly.

"Say," said the man, "aren't you feeling well? You look sick."

The flute climbed again and plucked cellos sounded below and the sea crept in and in toward the beach. Doc shook off the music, shook off the face, shook the chill out of his body. "Is there a police station near?"

"Up in town. Why, what's wrong?"

"There's a body out on the reef."

"Where?"

"Right out there—wedged between two rocks. A girl."

"Say—" said the man. "You get a bounty for finding a body. I forget how much."

Doc stood up and gathered his equipment. "Will you report it? I'm not feelng well."

"Give you a shock, did it? Is it—bad? Rotten or eat up?"

Doc turned away. "You take the bounty," he said. "I don't want it." He started toward the car. Only the tiniest piping of the flute sounded in his head.

19

Probably nothing in the way of promotion Holman's Department Store ever did attracted so much favorable comment as the engagement of the flag-pole skater. Day after day, there he was up on his little round platform skating around and around and at night he could be seen up there too, dark against the sky so that everybody knew he didn't come down. It was generally agreed, however, that a steel rod came up through the center of the platform at night and he strapped himself to it. But he didn't sit down and no one minded the steel rod. People came from Jamesburg to see him and from down the coast as far as Grimes Point. Salinas people came over in droves and the Farmers Mercantile of that town put in a bid for the next appearance when the skater could attempt to break his own record and thus give the new world's record to Salinas. Since there weren't many flag-pole skaters and since this one was by far the best, he had for the last year gone about breaking his own world's record.

Holman's was delighted about the venture. They

had a white sale, a remnant sale, an aluminum sale, and a crockery sale all going at the same time. Crowds of people stood in the street watching the lone man on his platform.

His second day up, he sent down word that someone was shooting at him with an air gun. The display department used its head. It figured the angles and located the offender. It was old Doctor Merrivale hiding behind the curtains of his office, plugging away with a Daisy air rifle. They didn't denounce him and he promised to stop. He was very prominent in the Masonic Lodge.

Henri the painter kept his chair at Red Williams' service station. He worked out every possible philosophic approach to the situation and came to the conclusion that he would have to build a platform at home and try it himself. Everyone in the town was more or less affected by the skater. Trade fell off out of sight of him and got better the nearer you came to Holman's. Mack and the boys went up and looked for a moment and then went back to the Palace. They couldn't see that it made much sense.

Holman's set up a double bed in their window. When the skater broke the world's record he was going to come down and sleep right in the window without taking off his skates. The trade name of the mattress was on a little card at the foot of the bed.

Now in the whole town there was interest and discussion about this sporting event, but the most interesting question of all and the one that bothered the whole town was never spoken of. No one mentioned it and yet it was there haunting everyone. Mrs. Trolat wondered about it as she came out of the Scotch bak-

ery with a bag of sweet buns. Mr. Hall in men's fur-
nishings wondered about it. The three Willoughby
girls giggled whenever they thought of it. But no one
had the courage to bring it into the open.

Richard Frost, a high-strung and brilliant young
man, worried about it more than anyone else. It
haunted him. Wednesday night he worried and Thursday night he fidgeted. Friday night he got drunk and
had a fight with his wife. She cried for a while and
then pretended to be asleep. She heard him slip from
bed and go into the kitchen. He was getting another
drink. And then she heard him dress quietly and go
out. She cried some more then. It was very late. Mrs.
Frost was sure he was going down to Dora's Bear Flag.

Richard walked sturdily down the hill through the
pines until he came to Lighthouse Avenue. He turned
left and went up toward Holman's. He had the bottle in
his pocket and just before he came to the store he took
one more slug of it. The street lights were turned down
low. The town was deserted. Not a soul moved. Richard
stood in the middle of the street and looked up.

Dimly on top of the high mast he could see the
lonely figure of the skater. He took another drink. He
cupped his hand and called huskily, "Hey!" There was
no answer. "Hey!" he called louder and looked around
to see if the cops had come out of their place beside
the bank.

Down from the sky came a surly reply: "What do
you want?"

Richard cupped his hands again. "How—how do
you—go to the toilet?"

"I've got a can up here," said the voice.

Richard turned and walked back the way he had

come. He walked along Lighthouse and up through the pines and he came to his house and let himself in. As he undressed he knew his wife was awake. She bubbled a little when she was asleep. He got into bed and she made room for him.

"He's got a can up there," Richard said.

20

In mid-morning the Model T truck rolled triumphantly home to Cannery Row and hopped the gutter and creaked up through the weeds to its place behind Lee Chong's. The boys blocked up the front wheels, drained what gasoline was left into a five-gallon can, took their frogs and went wearily home to the Palace Flophouse. Then Mack made a ceremonious visit to Lee Chong while the boys got a fire going in the big stove. Mack thanked Lee with dignity for lending the truck. He spoke of the great success of the trip, of the hundreds of frogs taken. Lee smiled shyly and waited for the inevitable.

"We're in the chips," Mack said enthusiastically. "Doc pays us a nickel a frog and we got about a thousand."

Lee nodded. The price was standard. Everybody knew that.

"Doc's away," said Mack. "Jesus, is he gonna be happy when he sees all them frogs."

Lee nodded again. He knew Doc was away and he also knew where the conversation was going.

"Say, by the way," said Mack as though he had just thought of it. "We're a little bit short right now—" He managed to make it sound like a very unusual situation.

"No whiskey," said Lee Chong and he smiled.

Mack was outraged. "What would we want whiskey for? Why we got a gallon of the finest whiskey you ever laid a lip over—a whole full God damned running over gallon. By the way," he continued, "I and the boys would like to have you just step up for a snort with us. They told me to ask you."

In spite of himself Lee smiled with pleasure. They wouldn't offer it if they didn't have it.

"No," said Mack, "I'll lay it on the line. I and the boys are pretty short and we're pretty hungry. You know the price of frogs is twenty for a buck. Now Doc is away and we're hungry. So what we thought is this. We don't want to see you lose nothing so we'll make over to you twenty-five frogs for a buck. You got a five-frog profit there and nobody loses his shirt."

"No," said Lee. "No money."

"Well, hell, Lee, all we need is a little groceries. I'll tell you what—we want to give Doc a little party when he gets back. We got plenty of liquor but we'd like to get maybe some steaks, and stuff like that. He's such a nice guy. Hell, when your wife had that bad tooth, who gave her the laudanum?"

Mack had him. Lee was indebted to Doc—deeply indebted. What Lee was having trouble comprehending was how his indebtedness to Doc made it necessary that he give credit to Mack.

"We don't want you to have like a mortgage on frogs," Mack went on. "We will actually deliver right

into your hands twenty-five frogs for every buck of
groceries you let us have and you can come to the
party too."

Lee's mind nosed over the proposition like a mouse
in a cheese cupboard. He could find nothing wrong with
it. The whole thing was legitimate. Frogs *were* cash as
far as Doc was concerned, the price was standard and
Lee had a double profit. He had his five-frog margin
and also he had the grocery mark-up. The whole thing
hinged on whether they actually had any frogs.

"We go see flog," Lee said at last.

In front of the Palace he had a drink of the whiskey,
inspected the damp sacks of frogs, and agreed to the
transaction. He stipulated, however, that he would
take no dead frogs. Now Mack counted fifty frogs into
a can and walked back to the grocery with Lee and got
two dollars' worth of bacon and eggs and bread.

Lee, anticipating a brisk business, brought a big
packing case out and put it into the vegetable department. He emptied the fifty frogs into it and covered it
with a wet gunny sack to keep his charges happy.

And business was brisk. Eddie sauntered down and
bought two frogs' worth of Bull Durham. Jones was outraged a little later when the price of Coca-Cola went up
from one to two frogs. In fact bitterness arose as the day
wore on and prices went up. Steak, for instance—the
very best steak shouldn't have been more than ten frogs
a pound but Lee set it at twelve and a half. Canned
peaches were sky high, eight frogs for a No. 2 can. Lee
had a stranglehold on the consumers. He was pretty
sure that the Thrift Market or Holman's would not ap-
prove of this new monetary system. If the boys wanted
steak, they knew they had to pay Lee's prices. Feeling

ran high when Hazel, who had coveted a pair of yellow
silk arm bands for a long time, was told that if he didn't
want to pay thirty-five frogs for them he could go some-
where else. The poison of greed was already creeping
into the innocent and laudable merchandising agreement. Bitterness was piling up. But in Lee's packing
case the frogs were piling up too.

Financial bitterness could not eat too deeply into
Mack and the boys, for they were not mercantile men.
They did not measure their joy in goods sold, their
egos in bank balances, nor their loves in what they
cost. While they were mildly irritated that Lee was
taking them for an economic ride or perhaps hop, two
dollars' worth of bacon and eggs was in their stomachs
lying right on top of a fine slug of whiskey and right on
top of the breakfast was another slug of whiskey. And
they sat in their own chairs in their own house and
watched Darling learning to drink canned milk out of a
sardine can. Darling was and was destined to remain a
very happy dog, for in the group of five men there were
five distinct theories of dog training, theories which
clashed so that Darling never got any training at all.
From the first she was a precocious bitch. She slept on
the bed of the man who had given her the last bribe.
They really stole for her sometimes. They wooed her
away from one another. Occasionally all five agreed
that things had to change and that Darling must be
disciplined, but in the discussion of method the inten-
tion invariably drifted away. They were in love with
her. They found the little puddles she left on the floor
charming. They bored all their acquaintances with her
cuteness and they would have killed her with food if in
the end she hadn't had better sense than they.

Jones made her a bed in the grandfather clock but Darling never used it. She slept with one or another of them as the fancy moved her. She chewed the blankets, tore the mattresses, sprayed the feathers out of the pillows. She coquetted and played her owners against one another. They thought she was wonderful. Mack intended to teach her tricks and go in vaudeville and he didn't even housebreak her.

They sat in the afternoon, smoking, digesting, considering, and now and then having a delicate drink from the jug. And each time they warned that they must not take too much, for it was to be for Doc. They must not forget that for a minute.

"What time you figure he'll be back?" Eddie asked.

"Usually gets in about eight or nine o'clock," said Mack. "Now we got to figure when we're going to give it. I think we ought to give it tonight."

"Sure," the others agreed.

"Maybe he might be tired," Hazel suggested. "That's a long drive."

"Hell," said Jones, "nothing rests you like a good party. I've been so dog tired my pants was draggin' and then I've went to a party and felt fine."

"We got to do some real thinkin'," said Mack. "Where we going to give it—here?"

"Well, Doc, he likes his music. He's always got his phonograph going at a party. Maybe he'd be more happy if we give it over at his place."

"You got something there," said Mack. "But I figure it ought to be like a surprise party. And how we going to make like it's a party and not just us bringin' over a jug of whiskey?"

"How about decorations?" Hughie suggested. "Like Fourth of July or Halloween."

Mack's eyes looked off into space and his lips were parted. He could see it all. "Hughie," he said, "I think you got something there. I never would of thought you could do it, but by God you really rang a duck that time." His voice grew mellow and his eyes looked into the future. "I can just see it," he said. "Doc comes home. He's tired. He drives up. The place is all lit up. He thinks somebody's broke in. He goes up the stairs and by God the place has got the hell decorated out of it. There's crepe paper and there's favors and a big cake. Jesus, he'd know it was a party then. And it wouldn't be no little mouse fart party neither. And we're kind of hiding so for a minute he don't know who done it. And then we come out yelling. Can't you see his face? By God, Hughie, I don't know how you thought of it."

Hughie blushed. His conception had been much more conservative, based in fact on the New Year's party at La Ida, but if it was going to be like that why Hughie was willing to take credit. "I just thought it would be nice," he said.

"Well, it's a pretty nice thing," said Mack, "and I don't mind saying when the surprise kind of wears off, I'm going to tell Doc who thought it up." They leaned back and considered the thing. And in their minds the decorated laboratory looked like the conservatory at the Hotel del Monte. They had a couple more drinks, just to savor the plan.

Lee Chong kept a very remarkable store. For instance, most stores buy yellow and black crepe paper

and black paper cats, masks and papier-mâché pumpkins in October. There is a brisk business for Halloween and then these items disappear. Maybe they are
sold or thrown out, but you can't buy them say in
June. The same is true of Fourth of July equipment,
flags and bunting and skyrockets. Where are they in
January? Gone—no one knows where. This was not
Lee Chong's way. You could buy Valentines in No-
vember at Lee Chong's, shamrocks, hatchets and
paper cherry trees in August. He had firecrackers he
had laid up in 1920. One of the mysteries was where
he kept his stock since his was not a very large store.
He had bathing suits he had bought when long skirts
and black stockings and head bandanas were in style.
He had bicycle clips and tatting shuttles and Mah Jong
sets. He had badges that said "Remember the Maine"
and felt pennants commemorating "Fighting Bob." He
had mementos of the Panama Pacific International Ex-
position of 1915—little towers of jewels. And there
was one other unorthodoxy in Lee's way of doing business. He never had a sale, never reduced a price and
never remaindered. An article that cost thirty cents in
1912 still was thirty cents although mice and moths
might seem to some to have reduced its value. But
there was no question about it. If you wanted to deco-
rate a laboratory in a general way, not being specific
about the season but giving the impression of a cross
between Saturnalia and a pageant of the Flags of all
Nations, Lee Chong's was the place to go for your
stuff.

Mack and the boys knew that, but Mack said,
"Where we going to get a big cake? Lee hasn't got
nothing but them little bakery cakes."

Hughie had been so successful before he tried
again. "Why'n't Eddie bake a cake?" he suggested.
"Eddie used to be fry cook at the San Carlos for a
while."

The instant enthusiasm for the idea drove from
Eddie's brain the admission that he had never baked a
cake.

Mack put it on a sentimental basis besides. "It
would mean more to Doc," he said. "It wouldn't be
like no God damned old soggy bought cake. It would
have some heart in it."

As the afternoon and the whiskey went down the
enthusiasm rose. There were endless trips to Lee
Chong's. The frogs were gone from one sack and Lee's
packing case was getting crowded. By six o'clock they
had finished the gallon of whiskey and were buying
half pints of Old Tennis Shoes at fifteen frogs a crack,
but the pile of decorating materials was heaped on the
floor of the Palace Flophouse—miles of crepe paper
commemorating every holiday in vogue and some that
had been abandoned.

Eddie watched his stove like a mother hen. He was
baking a cake in the wash basin. The recipe was guaranteed not to fail by the company which made the
shortening. But from the first the cake had acted
strangely. When the batter was completed it writhed
and panted as though animals were squirming and
crawling inside it. Once in the oven it put up a bubble
like a baseball which grew tight and shiny and then
collapsed with a hissing sound. This left such a crater
that Eddie made a new batch of batter and filled in the
hole. And now the cake was behaving very curiously
for while the bottom was burning and sending out a

black smoke the top was rising and falling glueyly with a series of little explosions.

When Eddie finally put it out to cool, it looked like one of Bel Geddes' miniatures of a battlefield on a lava bed.

This cake was not fortunate, for while the boys were decorating the laboratory Darling ate what she could of it, was sick in it, and finally curled up in its still warm dough and went to sleep.

But Mack and the boys had taken the crepe paper, the masks, the broomsticks and paper pumpkins, the red, white, and blue bunting, and moved over the lot and across the street to the laboratory. They disposed of the last of the frogs for a quart of Old Tennis Shoes and two gallons of 49-cent wine.

"Doc is very fond of wine," said Mack. "I think he likes it even better than whiskey."

Doc never locked the laboratory. He went on the theory that anyone who really wanted to break in could easily do it, that people were essentially honest and that, finally, there wasn't much the average person would want to steal there anyway. The valuable things were books and records, surgical instruments and optical glass and such things that a practical working burglar wouldn't look at twice. His theory had been sound as far as burglars, snatch thieves, and kleptomaniacs were concerned, but it had been completely ineffective regarding his friends. Books were often "borrowed." No can of beans ever survived his absence and on several occasions, returning late, he had found guests in his bed.

The boys piled the decorations in the anteroom and then Mack stopped them. "What's going to make Doc happiest?" he asked.

"The party!" said Hazel.

"No," said Mack.

"The decorations?" Hughie suggested. He felt responsible for the decorations.

"No," said Mack, "the frogs. That's going to make him feel best of all. Any maybe by the time he gets here, Lee Chong might be closed and he can't even see his frogs until tomorrow. No, sir," Mack cried. "Them frogs ought to be right here, right in the middle of the room with a piece of bunting on it and a sign that says, 'Welcome Home, Doc.' "

The committee which visited Lee met with stern opposition. All sorts of possibilities suggested themselves to his suspicious brain. It was explained that he was going to be at the party so he could watch his property, that no one questioned that they were his. Mack wrote out a paper transferring the frogs to Lee in case there should be any question.

When his protests weakened a little they carried the packing case over to the laboratory, tacked red, white, and blue bunting over it, lettered the big sign with iodine on a card, and they started the decorating from there. They had finished the whiskey by now and they really felt in a party mood. They criss-crossed the crepe paper, and put the pumpkins up. Passers-by in the street joined the party and rushed over to Lee's to get more to drink. Lee Chong joined the party for a while but his stomach was notoriously weak and he got sick and had to go home. At eleven o'clock they fried the steaks and ate them. Someone digging through the records found an album of Count Basie and the great phonograph roared out. The noise could be heard from the boat works to La Ida. A group of customers from the Bear Flag mistook Western Biological for a rival house and charged up the stairs whooping with joy. They were evicted by the outraged hosts but only after a long, happy, and bloody battle that took out the front door and broke two windows. The crashing of jars was unpleasant. Hazel going through the kitchen to the toilet tipped the frying pan of hot grease on himself and the floor and was badly burned.

At one-thirty a drunk wandered in and passed a remark which was considered insulting to Doc. Mack hit him a clip which is still remembered and discussed. The man rose off his feet, described a small arc, and crashed through the packing case in among the frogs. Someone trying to change a record dropped the tone arm down and broke the crystal.

No one has studied the psychology of a dying party. It may be raging, howling, boiling, and then a fever sets in and a little silence and then quickly quickly it is gone, the guests go home or go to sleep or wander away to some other affair and they leave a dead body.

The lights blazed in the laboratory. The front door hung sideways by one hinge. The floor was littered with broken glass. Phonograph records, some broken, some only nicked, were strewn about. The plates with pieces of steak ends and coagulating grease were on the floor, on top of the bookcases, under the bed. Whiskey glasses lay sadly on their sides. Someone trying to climb the bookcases had pulled out a whole section of books and spilled them in broken-backed confusion on the floor. And it was empty, it was over.

Through the broken end of the packing case a frog hopped and sat feeling the air for danger and then another joined him. They could smell the fine damp cool air coming in the door and in through the broken windows. One of them sat on the fallen card which said "Welcome Home, Doc." And then the two hopped timidly toward the door.

For quite a while a little river of frogs hopped down the steps, a swirling, moving river. For quite a while Cannery Row crawled with frogs—was overrun with frogs. A taxi which brought a very late customer to the Bear Flag squashed five frogs in the street. But well before dawn they had all gone. Some found the sewer and some worked their way up the hill to the reservoir and some went into culverts and some only hid among the weeds in the vacant lot.

And the lights blazed in the quiet empty laboratory.

21

In the back room of the laboratory the white rats in their cages ran and skittered and squeaked. In the corner of a separate cage a mother rat lay over her litter of blind naked children and let them suckle and the mother stared about nervously and fiercely.

In the rattlesnake cage the snakes lay with their chins resting on their own coils and they stared straight ahead out of their scowling dusty black eyes. In another cage a Gila monster with a skin like a beaded bag reared slowly up and clawed heavily and sluggishly at the wire. The anemones in the aquaria blossomed open, with green and purple tentacles and pale green stomachs. The little sea water pump whirred softly and the needles of driven water hissed into the tanks forcing lines of bubbles under the surface.

It was the hour of the pearl. Lee Chong brought his garbage cans out to the curb. The bouncer stood on the porch of the Bear Flag and scratched his stomach. Sam Malloy crawled out of the boiler and sat on his wood block and looked at the lightening east. Over on

the rocks near Hopkins Marine Station the sea lions
barked monotonously. The old Chinaman came up out
of the sea with his dripping basket and flip-flapped up
the hill.

Then a car turned into Cannery Row and Doc drove
up to the front of the laboratory. His eyes were red
rimmed with fatigue. He moved slowly with tiredness.
When the car had stopped, he sat still for a moment to
let the road jumps get out of his nerves. Then he
climbed out of the car. At his step on the stairs, the
rattlesnakes ran out their tongues and listened with
their waving forked tongues. The rats scampered
madly about the cages. Doc climbed the stairs. He
looked in wonder at the sagging door and at the broken
window. The weariness seemed to go out of him. He
stepped quickly inside. Then he went quickly from
room to room, stepping around the broken glass. He
bent down quickly and picked up a smashed phonograph record and looked at its title.

In the kitchen the spilled grease had turned white
on the floor. Doc's eyes flamed red with anger. He sat
down on his couch and his head settled between his
shoulders and his body weaved a little in his rage.
Suddenly he jumped up and turned on the power in his
great phonograph. He put on a record and put down
the arm. Only a hissing roar came from the loud-
speaker. He lifted the arm, stopped the turntable, and
sat down on the couch again.

On the stairs there were bumbling uncertain footsteps and through the door came Mack. His face was
red. He stood uncertainly in the middle of the room.
"Doc—" he said— "I and the boys—"

For the moment Doc hadn't seemed to see him. Now

he leaped to his feet. Mack shuffled backward. "Did you do this?"

"Well, I and the boys—" Doc's small hard fist whipped out and splashed against Mack's mouth. Doc's eyes shone with a red animal rage. Mack sat down heavily on the floor. Doc's fist was hard and sharp. Mack's lips were split against his teeth and one front tooth bent sharply inward. "Get up!" said Doc.

Mack lumbered to his feet. His hands were at his sides. Doc hit him again, a cold calculated punishing punch in the mouth. The blood spurted from Mack's lips and ran down his chin. He tried to lick his lips.

"Put up your hands. Fight, you son of a bitch," Doc cried, and he hit him again and heard the crunch of breaking teeth.

Mack's head jolted but he was braced now so he wouldn't fall. And his hands stayed at his sides. "Go ahead, Doc," he said thickly through his broken lips. "I got it coming."

Doc's shoulders sagged with defeat. "You son of a bitch," he said bitterly. "Oh you dirty son of a bitch." He sat down on the couch and looked at his cut knuckles.

Mack sat down in a chair and looked at him. Mack's eyes were wide and full of pain. He didn't even wipe away the blood that flowed down his chin. In Doc's head the monotonal opening of Monteverdi's *Hor ch' el Ciel e la Terra* began to form, the infinitely sad and resigned mourning of Petrarch for Laura. Doc saw Mack's broken mouth through the music, the music that was in his head and in the air. Mack sat perfectly still, almost as though he could hear the music too. Doc glanced at the place where the Monteverdi album was and then he remembered that the phonograph was broken.

He got to his feet. "Go wash your face," he said and he went out and down the stairs and across the street to Lee Chong's. Lee wouldn't look at him as he got two quarts of beer out of the icebox. He took the money without saying anything. Doc walked back across the street.

Mack was in the toilet cleaning his bloody face with wet paper towels. Doc opened a bottle and poured gently into a glass, holding it at an angle so that very little collar rose to the top. He filled a second tall glass and carried the two into the front room. Mack came back dabbing at his mouth with wet towelling. Doc indicated the beer with his head. Now Mack opened his throat and poured down half the glass without swallowing. He sighed explosively and stared into the beer. Doc had already finished his glass. He brought the bottle in and filled both glasses again. He sat down on his couch.

"What happened?" he asked.

Mack looked at the floor and a drop of blood fell from his lips into his beer. He mopped his split lips again. "I and the boys wanted to give you a party. We thought you'd be home last night."

Doc nodded his head. "I see."

"She got out of hand," said Mack. "It don't do no good to say I'm sorry. I been sorry all my life. This ain't no new thing. It's always like this." He swallowed deeply from his glass. "I had a wife," Mack said. "Same thing. Ever'thing I done turned sour. She couldn't stand it any more. If I done a good thing it got poisoned up some way. If I give her a present they was something wrong with it. She only got hurt from me. She couldn't stand it no more. Same thing ever' place 'til I just got to clowning. I don't do nothin' but clown no more. Try to make the boys laugh."

Doc nodded again. The music was sounding in his head again, complaint and resignation all in one. "I know," he said.

"I was glad when you hit me," Mack went on. "I thought to myself—'Maybe this will teach me. Maybe I'll remember this.' But, hell, I won't remember nothin'. I won't learn nothin'. Doc," Mack cried, "the way I seen it, we was all happy and havin' a good time. You was glad because we was givin' you a party. And we was glad. The way I seen it, it was a good party." He waved his hand at the wreckage on the floor. "Same thing when I was married. I'd think her out and then——but it never come off that way."

"I know," said Doc. He opened the second quart of beer and poured the glasses full.

"Doc," said Mack, "I and the boys will clean up here—and we'll pay for the stuff that's broke. If it takes us five years we'll pay for it."

Doc shook his head slowly and wiped the beer foam from his mustache. "No," he said, "I'll clean it up. I know where everything goes."

"We'll pay for it, Doc."

"No you won't, Mack," said Doc. "You'll think about it and it'll worry you for quite a long time, but you won't pay for it. There's maybe three hundred dollars in broken museum glass. Don't say you'll pay for it. That will just keep you uneasy. It might be two or three years before you forgot about it and felt entirely easy again. And you wouldn't pay it anyway."

"I guess you're right," said Mack. "God damn it, I *know* you're right. What can we do?"

"I'm over it," said Doc. "Those socks in the mouth got it out of my system. Let's forget it."

Mack finished his beer and stood up. "So long, Doc," he said.

"So long. Say, Mack—what happened to your wife?"

"I don't know," said Mack. "She went away." He walked clumsily down the stairs and crossed over and walked up the lot and up the chicken walk to the Palace Flophouse. Doc watched his progress through the window. And then wearily he got a broom from behind the water heater. It took him all day to clean up the mess.

22

Henri the painter was not French and his name was not Henri. Also he was not really a painter. Henri had so steeped himself in stories of the Left Bank in Paris that he lived there although he had never been there. Feverishly he followed in periodicals the Dadaist movements and schisms, the strangely feminine jealousies and religiousness, the obscurantisms of the forming and breaking schools. Regularly he revolted against outworn techniques and materials. One season he threw out perspective. Another year he abandoned red, even as the mother of purple. Finally he gave up paint entirely. It is not known whether Henri was a good painter or not for he threw himself so violently into movements that he had very little time left for painting of any kind.

About his painting there is some question. You couldn't judge very much from his productions in different colored chicken feathers and nutshells. But as a boat builder he was superb. Henri was a wonderful craftsman. He had lived in a tent years ago when he started his boat and until galley and cabin were complete enough to move into. But once he was housed and dry he had taken his time on the boat. The boat was sculptured rather than built. It was thirty-five feet long and its lines were in a constant state of flux. For a while it had a clipper bow and a fantail like a destroyer. Another time it had looked vaguely like a caravel. Since Henri had no money, it sometimes took him months to find a plank or a piece of iron or a dozen brass screws. That was the way he wanted it, for Henri never wanted to finish his boat.

It sat among the pine trees on a lot Henri rented for five dollars a year. This paid the taxes and satisfied the owner. The boat rested in a cradle on concrete foundations. A rope ladder hung over the side except when Henri was at home. Then he pulled up the rope ladder and only put it down when guests arrived. His little cabin had a wide padded seat that ran around three sides of the room. On this he slept and on this his guests sat. A table folded down when it was needed and a brass lamp hung from the ceiling. His galley was a marvel of compactness but every item in it had been the result of months of thought and work.

Henri was swarthy and morose. He wore a beret long after other people abandoned them, he smoked a calabash pipe and his dark hair fell about his face. Henri had many friends whom he loosely classified as those who could feed him and those whom he had to feed. His boat had no name. Henri said he would name it when it was finished.

Henri had been living in and building his boat for ten years. During that time he had been married twice and had promoted a number of semi-permanent liai-

sons. And all of these young women had left him for
the same reason. The seven-foot cabin was too small
for two people. They resented bumping their heads
when they stood up and they definitely felt the need
for a toilet. Marine toilets obviously would not work in
a shore-bound boat and Henri refused to compromise
with a spurious landsman's toilet. He and his friend of
the moment had to stroll away among the pines. And
one after another his loves left him.

Just after the girl he had called Alice left him, a
very curious thing happened to Henri. Each time he
was left alone, he mourned formally for a while but
actually he felt a sense of relief. He could stretch out
in his little cabin. He could eat what he wanted. He
was glad to be free of the endless female biologic
functions for a while.

It had become his custom, each time he was deserted, to buy a gallon of wine, to stretch out on the
comfortably hard bunk and get drunk. Sometimes he
cried a little all by himself but it was luxurious stuff
and he usually had a wonderful feeling of well-being
from it. He would read Rimbaud aloud with a very bad
accent, marveling the while at his fluid speech.

It was during one of his ritualistic mournings for the
lost Alice that the strange thing began to happen. It
was night and his lamp was burning and he had just
barely begun to get drunk when suddenly he knew he
was no longer alone. He let his eye wander cautiously
up and across the cabin and there on the other side sat
a devilish young man, a dark handsome young man.
His eyes gleamed with cleverness and spirit and en-
ergy and his teeth flashed. There was something very
dear and yet very terrible in his face. And beside him

sat a golden-haired little boy, hardly more than a baby. The man looked down at the baby and the baby looked back and laughed delightedly as though something wonderful were about to happen. Then the man looked over at Henri and smiled and he glanced back at the baby. From his upper left vest pocket he took an old-fashioned straight-edged razor. He opened it and indicated the child with a gesture of his head. He put a hand among the curls and the baby laughed gleefully and then the man tilted the chin and cut the baby's throat and the baby went right on laughing. But Henri was howling with terror. It took him a long time to realize that neither the man nor the baby was still there.

Henri, when his shaking had subsided a little, rushed out of his cabin, leaped over the side of the boat and hurried away down the hill through the pines. He walked for several hours and at last he walked down to Cannery Row.

Doc was in the basement working on cats when Henri burst in. Doc went on working while Henri told about it and when it was over Doc looked closely at him to see how much actual fear and how much theater was there. And it was mostly fear.

"Is it a ghost do you think?" Henri demanded. "Is it some reflection of something that has happened or is it some Freudian horror out of me or am I completely nuts? I saw it, I tell you. It happened right in front of me as plainly as I see you."

"I don't know," said Doc.

"Well, will you come up with me, and see if it comes back?"

"No," said Doc. "If I saw it, it might be a ghost and

it would scare me badly because I don't believe in ghosts. And if you saw it again and I didn't it would be a hallucination and you would be frightened."

"But what am I going to do?" Henri asked. "If I see it again I'll know what's going to happen and I'm sure I'll die. You see he doesn't look like a murderer. He looks nice and the kid looks nice and neither of them give a damn. But he cut that baby's throat. I saw it."

"I don't know," said Doc. "I'm not a psychiatrist or a witch hunter and I'm not going to start now."

A girl's voice called into the basement. "Hi, Doc, can I come in?"

"Come along," said Doc.

She was a rather pretty and a very alert girl.

Doc introduced her to Henri.

"He's got a problem," said Doc. "He either has a ghost or a terrible conscience and he doesn't know which. Tell her about it, Henri."

Henri went over the story again and the girl's eyes sparkled.

"But that's horrible," she said when he finished. "I've never in my life even caught the smell of a ghost. Let's go back up and see if he comes again."

Doc watched them go a little sourly. After all it had been his date.

The girl never did see the ghost but she was fond of Henri and it was five months before the cramped cabin and the lack of a toilet drove her out.

23

A black gloom settled over the Palace Flophouse. All the joy went out of it. Mack came back from the laboratory with his mouth torn and his teeth broken. As a kind of penance, he did not wash his face. He went to his bed and pulled his blanket over his head and he didn't get up all day. His heart was as bruised as his mouth. He went over all the bad things he had done in his life and everything he had ever done seemed bad. He was very sad.

Hughie and Jones sat for a while staring into space and then morosely they went over to the Hediondo Cannery and applied for jobs and got them.

Hazel felt so bad that he walked to Monterey and picked a fight with a soldier and lost it on purpose. That made him feel a little better to be utterly beaten by a man Hazel could have licked without half trying.

Darling was the only happy one of the whole club. She spent the day under Mack's bed happily eating up his shoes. She was a clever dog and her teeth were very sharp. Twice in his black despair, Mack reached under the bed and caught her and put her in bed with him for company but she squirmed out and went back to eating his shoes.

Eddie mooned on down to La Ida and talked to his friend the bartender. He got a few drinks and borrowed some nickels with which he played *Melancholy Baby* five times on the juke box.

Mack and the boys were under a cloud and they knew it and they knew they deserved it. They had become social outcasts. All of their good intentions were forgotten now. The fact that the party was given for Doc, if it was known, was never mentioned or taken into consideration. The story ran through the Bear Flag. It was told in the canneries. At La Ida drunks discussed it virtuously. Lee Chong refused to comment. He was feeling financially bruised. And the story as it grew went this way: They had stolen liquor and money. They had maliciously broken into the laboratory and systematically destroyed it out of pure malice and evil. People who really knew better took this view. Some of the drunks at La Ida considered going over and beating the hell out of the whole lot of them to show them they couldn't do a thing like that to Doc.

Only a sense of the solidarity and fighting ability of Mack and the boys saved them from some kind of reprisal. There were people who felt virtuous about the affair who hadn't had the material of virtue for a long time. The fiercest of the whole lot was Tom Sheligan who would have been at the party if he had known about it.

Socially Mack and the boys were beyond the pale. Sam Malloy didn't speak to them as they went by the boiler. They drew into themselves and no one could foresee how they would come out of the cloud. For

there are two possible reactions to social ostracism—
either a man emerges determined to be better, purer,
and kindlier or he goes bad, challenges the world and
does even worse things. This last is by far the commonest reaction to stigma.

Mack and the boys balanced on the scales of good
and evil. They were kind and sweet to Darling; they
were forbearing and patient with one another. When
the first reaction was over they gave the Palace Flophouse a cleaning such as it had never had. They polished the bright work on the stove and they washed all
their clothes and blankets. Financially they had become dull and solvent. Hughie and Jones were working and bringing home their pay. They bought groceries up the hill at the Thrift Market because they could
not stand the reproving eyes of Lee Chong.

It was during this time that Doc made an observa-
tion which may have been true, but since there was
one factor missing in his reasoning it is not known
whether he was correct. It was the Fourth of July. Doc
was sitting in the laboratory with Richard Frost. They
drank beer and listened to a new album of Scarlatti
and looked out the window. In front of the Palace
Flophouse there was a large log of wood where Mack
and the boys were sitting in the mid-morning sun.
They faced down the hill toward the laboratory.

Doc said, "Look at them. There are your true phi-
losophers. I think," he went on, "that Mack and the
boys know everything that has ever happened in the
world and possibly everything that will happen. I think
they survive in this particular world better than other
people. In a time when people tear themselves to
pieces with ambition and nervousness and covetous-

ness, they are relaxed. All of our so-called successful
men are sick men, with bad stomachs, and bad souls,
but Mack and the boys are healthy and curiously
clean. They can do what they want. They can satisfy
their appetites without calling them something else."
This speech so dried out Doc's throat that he drained
his beer glass. He waved two fingers in the air and
smiled. "There's nothing like that first taste of beer,"
he said.

Richard Frost said, "I think they're just like anyone
else. They just haven't any money."

"They could get it," Doc said. "They could ruin
their lives and get money. Mack has qualities of ge-
nius. They're all very clever if they want something.
They just know the nature of things too well to be
caught in that wanting."

If Doc had known of the sadness of Mack and the
boys he would not have made the next statement, but
no one had told him about the social pressure that was
exerted against the inmates of the Palace.

He poured beer slowly into his glass. "I think I can
show you proof," he said. "You see how they are sitting facing this way? Well—in about half an hour the
Fourth of July Parade is going to pass on Lighthouse
Avenue. By just turning their heads they can see it, by
standing up they can watch it, and by walking two
short blocks they can be right beside it. Now I'll bet
you a quart of beer they won't even turn their heads."

"Suppose they don't?" said Richard Frost. "What
will that prove?"

"What will it prove?" cried Doc. "Why just that
they know what will be in the parade. They will know

that the Mayor will ride first in an automobile with
bunting streaming back from the hood. Next will come
Long Bob on his white horse with the flag. Then the
city council, then two companies of soldiers from the
Presidio, next the Elks with purple umbrellas, then
the Knights Templar in white ostrich feathers and carrying swords. Next the Knights of Columbus with red
ostrich feathers and carrying swords. Mack and the
boys know that. The band will play. They've seen it
all. They don't have to look again."

"The man doesn't live who doesn't have to look at a
parade," said Richard Frost.

"Is it a bet then?"

"It's a bet."

"It has always seemed strange to me," said Doc.
"The things we admire in men, kindness and generos-
ity, openness, honesty, understanding and feeling are
the concomitants of failure in our system. And those
traits we detest, sharpness, greed, acquisitiveness,
meanness, egotism and self-interest are the traits of
success. And while men admire the quality of the first
they love the produce of the second."

"Who wants to be good if he has to be hungry too?"
said Richard Frost.

"Oh, it isn't a matter of hunger. It's something quite
different. The sale of souls to gain the whole world is
completely voluntary and almost unanimous—but not
quite. Everywhere in the world there are Mack and the
boys. I've seen them in an ice-cream seller in Mexico
and in an Aleut in Alaska. You know how they tried to
give me a party and something went wrong. But they
wanted to give me a party. That was their impulse.

Listen," said Doc. "Isn't that the band I hear?"
Quickly he filled two glasses with beer and the two of
them stepped close to the window.

Mack and the boys sat dejectedly on their log and
faced the laboratory. The sound of the band came from
Lighthouse Avenue, the drums echoing back from the
buildings. And suddenly the Mayor's car crossed and
it sprayed bunting from the radiator—then Long Bob
on his white horse carrying the flag, then the band,
then the soldiers, the Elks, the Knights Templar, the
Knights of Columbus. Richard and the Doc leaned
forward tensely but they were watching the line of men
sitting on the log.

And not a head turned, not a neck straightened up.
The parade filed past and they did not move. And the
parade was gone. Doc drained his glass and waved two
fingers gently in the air and he said, "Hah! There's
nothing in the world like that first taste of beer."

Richard started for the door. "What kind of beer do
you want?"

"The same kind," said Doc gently. He was smiling
up the hill at Mack and the boys.

It's all fine to say, "Time will heal everything, this
too shall pass away. People will forget"—and things
like that when you are not involved, but when you are
there is no passage of time, people do not forget and
you are in the middle of something that does not
change. Doc didn't know the pain and self-destructive
criticism in the Palace Flophouse or he might have
tried to do something about it. And Mack and the boys
did not know how he felt or they would have held up
their heads again.

It was a bad time. Evil stalked darkly in the vacant

lot. Sam Malloy had a number of fights with his wife
and she cried all the time. The echoes inside the
boiler made it sound as though she were crying under
water. Mack and the boys seemed to be the node of
trouble. The nice bouncer at the Bear Flag threw out a
drunk, but threw him too hard and too far and broke
his back. Alfred had to go over to Salinas three times
before it was cleared up and that didn't make Alfred
feel very well. Ordinarily he was too good a bouncer to
hurt anyone. His A and C was a miracle of rhythm and
grace.

On top of that a group of high-minded ladies in the
town demanded that dens of vice must close to protect
young American manhood. This happened about once
a year in the dead period between the Fourth of July
and the County Fair. Dora usually closed the Bear
Flag for a week when it happened. It wasn't so bad.
Everyone got a vacation and little repairs to the
plumbing and the walls could be made. But this year
the ladies went on a real crusade. They wanted somebody's scalp. It had been a dull summer and they were
restless. It got so bad that they had to be told who
actually owned the property where vice was practiced,
what the rents were and what little hardships might be
the result of their closing. That was how close they
were to being a serious menace.

Dora was closed a full two weeks and there were
three conventions in Monterey while the Bear Flag was
closed. Word got around and Monterey lost five conventions for the following year. Things were bad all
over. Doc had to get a loan at the bank to pay for the
glass that was broken at the party. Elmer Rechati went
to sleep on the Southern Pacific track and lost both

legs. A sudden and completely unexpected storm tore a purse-seiner and three lampara boats loose from their moorings and tossed them broken and sad on Del Monte beach.

There is no explaining a series of misfortunes like that. Every man blames himself. People in their black minds remember sins committed secretly and wonder whether they have caused the evil sequence. One man may put it down to sun spots while another invoking the law of probabilities doesn't believe it. Not even the doctors had a good time of it, for while many people were sick none of it was good-paying sickness. It was nothing a good physic or a patent medicine wouldn't take care of.

And to cap it all, Darling got sick. She was a very fat and lively puppy when she was struck down, but five days of fever reduced her to a little skin-covered skeleton. Her liver-colored nose was pink and her gums were white. Her eyes glazed with illness and her whole body was hot although she trembled sometimes with cold. She wouldn't eat and she wouldn't drink and her fat little belly shriveled up against her spine, and even her tail showed the articulations through the skin. It was obviously distemper.

Now a genuine panic came over the Palace Flophouse. Darling had come to be vastly important to them. Hughie and Jones instantly quit their jobs so they could be near to help. They sat up in shifts. They kept a cool damp cloth on her forehead and she got weaker and sicker. Finally, although they didn't want to, Hazel and Jones were chosen to call on Doc. They found him working over a tide chart while he ate a chicken stew of which the principal ingredient was not chicken but sea cucumber. They thought he looked at them a little coldly.

"It's Darling," they said. "She's sick."

"What's the matter with her?"

"Mack says it's distemper."

"I'm no veterinarian," said Doc. "I don't know how to treat these things."

Hazel said, "Well, couldn't you just take a look at her? She's sick as hell."

They stood in a circle while Doc examined Darling. He looked at her eyeballs and her gums and felt in her ear for fever. He ran his finger over the ribs that stuck out like spokes and at the poor spine. "She won't eat?" he asked.

"Not a thing," said Mack.

"You'll have to force feed her—strong soup and eggs and cod liver oil."

They thought he was cold and professional. He went back to his tide charts and his stew.

But Mack and the boys had something to do now. They boiled meat until it was as strong as whiskey. They put cod liver oil far back on her tongue so that some of it got down her. They held up her head and made a little funnel of her chops and poured the cool soup in. She had to swallow or drown. Every two hours they fed her and gave her water. Before they had slept in shifts—now no one slept. They sat silently and waited for Darling's crisis.

It came early in the morning. The boys sat in their chairs half asleep but Mack was awake and his eyes were on the puppy. He saw her ears flip twice, and her

chest heave. With infinite weakness she climbed
slowly to her spindly legs, dragged herself to the door,
took four laps of water and collapsed on the floor.

Mack shouted the others awake. He danced heavily.
All the boys shouted at one another. Lee Chong heard
them and snorted to himself as he carried out the
garbage cans. Alfred the bouncer heard them and
thought they were having a party.

By nine o'clock Darling had eaten a raw egg and
half a pint of whipped cream by herself. By noon she
was visibly putting on weight. In a day she romped a
little and by the end of the week she was a well dog.

At last a crack had developed in the wall of evil.
There were evidences of it everywhere. The purse-
seiner was hauled back into the water and floated.
Word came down to Dora that it was all right to open
up the Bear Flag. Earl Wakefield caught a sculpin
with two heads and sold it to the museum for eight
dollars. The wall of evil and of waiting was broken. It
broke away in chunks. The curtains were drawn at the
laboratory that night and Gregorian music played until
two o'clock and then the music stopped and no one
came out. Some force wrought with Lee Chong's heart
and all in an Oriental moment he forgave Mack and
the boys and wrote off the frog debt which had been a
monetary headache from the beginning. And to prove
to the boys that he had forgiven them he took a pint of
Old Tennis Shoes up and presented it to them. Their
trading at the Thrift Market had hurt his feelings but it
was all over now. Lee's visit coincided with the first
destructive healthy impulse Darling had since her illness. She was completely spoiled now and no one
thought of housebreaking her. When Lee Chong came

in with his gift, Darling was deliberately and happily destroying Hazel's only pair of rubber boots while her happy masters applauded her.

Mack never visited the Bear Flag professionally. It would have seemed a little like incest to him. There was a house out by the baseball park he patronized. Thus, when he went into the front bar, everyone thought he wanted a beer. He stepped up to Alfred. "Dora around?" he asked.

"What do you want with her?" Alfred asked.

"I got something I want to ask her."

"What about?"

"That's none of your God damn business," said Mack.

"Okay. Have it your way. I'll see if she wants to talk to you."

A moment later he led Mack into the sanctum. Dora sat at a rolltop desk. Her orange hair was piled in ringlets on her head and she wore a green eyeshade. With a stub pen she was bringing her books up to date, a fine old double entry ledger. She was dressed in a magnificent pink silk wrapper with lace at the wrists and throat. When Mack came in she whirled her pivot chair about and faced him. Alfred stood in the door and waited. Mack stood until Alfred closed the door and left.

Dora scrutinized him suspiciously. "Well—what can I do for you?" she demanded at last.

"You see, ma'am," said Mack— "Well I guess you heard what we done over at Doc's some time back."

Dora pushed the eyeshade back up on her head and she put the pen in an old-fashioned coil-spring holder. "Yeah!" she said. "I heard."

"Well, ma'am, we did it for Doc. You may not believe it but we wanted to give him a party. Only he didn't get home in time and—well she got out of hand."

"So I heard," said Dora. "Well, what you want me to do?"

"Well," said Mack, "I and the boys thought we'd ask you. You know what we think of Doc. We wanted to ask you what you thought we could do for him that would kind of show him."

Dora said, "Hum," and she flopped back in her pivot chair and crossed her legs and smoothed her wrapper over her knees. She shook out a cigarette, lighted it and studied. "You gave him a party he didn't get to. Why don't you give him a party he does get to?" she said.

"Jesus," said Mack afterwards talking to the boys. "It was just as simple as that. Now there is one hell of a woman. No wonder she got to be a madam. There is one hell of a woman."

24

Mary Talbot, Mrs. Tom Talbot, that is, was lovely. She had red hair with green lights in it. Her skin was golden with a green undercast and her eyes were green with little golden spots. Her face was triangular, with wide cheekbones, wide-set eyes, and her chin was pointed. She had long dancer's legs and dancer's feet and she seemed never to touch the ground when she walked. When she was excited, and she was excited a good deal of the time, her face flushed with gold. Her great-great-great-great-great grandmother had been burned as a witch.

More than anything in the world Mary Talbot loved parties. She loved to give parties and she loved to go to parties. Since Tom Talbot didn't make much money Mary couldn't give parties all the time so she tricked people into giving them. Sometimes she telephoned a friend and said bluntly, "Isn't it about time you gave a party?"

Regularly Mary had six birthdays a year, and she organized costume parties, surprise parties, holiday parties. Christmas Eve at her house was a very excit-

ing thing. For Mary glowed with parties. She carried
her husband Tom along on the wave of her excitement.

In the afternoons when Tom was at work Mary sometimes gave tea parties for the neighborhood cats. She
set a footstool with doll cups and saucers. She gathered the cats, and there were plenty of them, and then
she held long and detailed conversations with them. It
was a kind of play she enjoyed very much—a kind of
satiric game and it covered and concealed from Mary
the fact that she didn't have very nice clothes and the
Talbots didn't have any money. They were pretty near
absolute bottom most of the time, and when they really
scraped, Mary managed to give some kind of a party.

She could do that. She could infect a whole house
with gaiety and she used her gift as a weapon against
the despondency that lurked always around outside the
house waiting to get in at Tom. That was Mary's job as
she saw it—to keep the despondency away from Tom
because everyone knew he was going to be a great
success some time. Mostly she was successful in keeping the dark things out of the house but sometimes
they got in at Tom and laid him out. Then he would sit
and brood for hours while Mary frantically built up a
backfire of gaiety.

One time when it was the first of the month and
there were curt notes from the water company and the
rent wasn't paid and a manuscript had come back from
Collier's and the cartoons had come back from *The
New Yorker* and pleurisy was hurting Tom pretty badly,
he went into the bedroom and lay down on the bed.

Mary came softly in, for the blue-gray color of his
gloom had seeped out under the door and through the

keyhole. She had a little bouquet of candy tuft in a collar of paper lace.

"Smell," she said and held the bouquet to his nose. He smelled the flowers and said nothing. "Do you know what day this is?" she asked and thought wildly for something to make it a bright day.

Tom said, "Why don't we face it for once? We're down. We're going under. What's the good of kidding ourselves?"

"No we're not," said Mary. "We're magic people. We always have been. Remember that ten dollars you found in a book—remember when your cousin sent you five dollars? Nothing can happen to us."

"Well, it has happened," said Tom. "I'm sorry," he said. "I just can't talk myself out of it this time. I'm sick of pretending everything. For once I'd like to have it real—just for once."

"I thought of giving a little party tonight," said Mary.

"On what? You're not going to cut out the baked ham picture from a magazine again and serve it on a platter, are you? I'm sick of that kind of kidding. It isn't funny any more. It's sad."

"I could give a little party," she insisted. "Just a small affair. Nobody will dress. It's the anniversary of the founding of the Bloomer League—you didn't even remember that."

"It's no use," said Tom. "I know it's mean but I just can't rise to it. Why don't you just go out and shut the door and leave me alone? I'll get you down if you don't."

She looked at him closely and saw that he meant it.

Mary walked quietly out and shut the door, and Tom turned over on the bed and put his face down between his arms. He could hear her rustling about in the other room.

She decorated the door with old Christmas things, glass balls, and tinsel, and she made a placard that said "Welcome Tom, our Hero." She listened at the door and couldn't hear anything. A little disconsolately she got out the footstool and spread a napkin over it. She put her bouquet in a glass in the middle of the footstool and set out four little cups and saucers. She went into the kitchen, put the tea in the teapot and set the kettle to boil. Then she went out into the yard.

Kitty Randolph was sunning herself by the front fence. Mary said, "Miss Randolph—I'm having a few friends in to tea if you would care to come." Kitty Randolph rolled over languorously on her back and stretched in the warm sun. "Don't be later than four o'clock," said Mary. "My husband and I are going to the Bloomer League Centennial Reception at the Hotel."

She strolled around the house to the backyard where the blackberry vines clambered over the fence. Kitty Casini was squatting was squatting on the ground growling to herself and flicking her tail fiercely. "Mrs. Casini," Mary began and then she stopped for she saw what the cat was doing. Kitty Casini had a mouse. She patted it gently with her unarmed paw and the mouse squirmed horribly away dragging its paralyzed hind legs behind it. The cat let it get nearly to the cover of the blackberry vines and then she reached delicately out and white thorns had sprouted on her paw. Daintily she stabbed the mouse through the back and drew it wriggling to her and her tail flicked with tense delight.

Tom must have been at least half asleep when he heard his name called over and over. He jumped up shouting, "What is it? Where are you?" He could hear Mary crying. He ran out into the yard and saw what was happening. "Turn your head," he shouted and he killed the mouse. Kitty Casini had leaped to the top of the fence where she watched him angrily. Tom picked up a rock and hit her in the stomach and knocked her off the fence.

In the house Mary was still crying a little. She poured the water into the teapot and brought it to the table. "Sit there," she told Tom and he squatted down on the floor in front of the footstool.

"Can't I have a big cup?" he asked.

"I can't blame Kitty Casini," said Mary. "I know how cats are. It isn't her fault. But—Oh, Tom! I'm going to have trouble inviting her again. I'm just not going to like her for a while no matter how much I want to." She looked closely at Tom and saw that the lines were gone from his forehead and that he was not blinking badly. "But then I'm so busy with the Bloomer League these days," she said, "I just don't know how I'm going to get everything done."

Mary Talbot gave a pregnancy party that year. And everyone said, "God! A kid of hers is going to have fun."

25

Certainly all of Cannery Row and probably all of Monterey felt that a change had come. It's all right not to believe in luck and omens. Nobody believes in them. But it doesn't do any good to take chances with them and no one takes chances. Cannery Row, like every place else, is not superstitious but will not walk under a ladder or open an umbrella in the house. Doc was a pure scientist and incapable of superstition and yet when he came in late one night and found a line of white flowers across the doorsill he had a bad time of it. But most people in Cannery Row simply do not believe in such things and then live by them.

There was no doubt in Mack's mind that a dark cloud had hung on the Palace Flophouse. He had analyzed the abortive party and found that a misfortune had crept into every crevice, that bad luck had come up like hives on the evening. And once you got into a routine like that the best thing to do was just to go to bed until it was over. You couldn't buck it. Not that Mack was superstitious.

Now a kind of gladness began to penetrate into the Row and to spread out from there. Doc was almost supernaturally successful with a series of lady visitors. He didn't half try. The puppy at the Palace was growing like a pole bean, and having a thousand generations of training behind her, she began to train herself. She got disgusted with wetting on the floor and took to going outside. It was obvious that Darling was going to grow up a good and charming dog. And she had developed no chorea from her distemper.

The benignant influence crept like gas through the Row. It got as far as Herman's hamburger stand, it spread to the San Carlos Hotel. Jimmy Brucia felt it and Johnny his singing bartender. Sparky Evea felt it and joyously joined battle with three new out of town cops. It even got as far as the County Jail in Salinas where Gay, who had lived a good life by letting the sheriff beat him at checkers, suddenly grew cocky and never lost another game. He lost his privileges that way but he felt a whole man again.

The sea lions felt it and their barking took on a tone and a cadence that would have gladdened the heart of St. Francis. Little girls studying their catechism suddenly looked up and giggled for no reason at all. Perhaps some electrical finder could have been developed so delicate that it could have located the source of all this spreading joy and fortune. And triangulation might possibly have located it in the Palace Flophouse and Grill. Certainly the Palace was lousy with it. Mack and the boys were charged. Jones was seen to leap from his chair only to do a quick tap dance and sit down again. Hazel smiled vaguely at nothing at all. The joy was so general and so suffused that Mack had

a hard time keeping it centered and aimed at its objec-
tive. Eddie who had worked at La Ida pretty regularly
was accumulating a cellar of some promise. He no
longer added beer to the wining jug. It gave a flat taste
to the mixture, he said.

Sam Malloy had planted morning glories to grow
over the boiler. He had put out a little awning and
under it he and his wife often sat in the evening. She
was crocheting a bedspread.

The joy even got into the Bear Flag. Business was
good. Phyllis Mae's leg was knitting nicely and she
was nearly ready to go to work again. Eva Flanegan got
back from East St. Louis very glad to be back. It had
been hot in East St. Louis and it hadn't been as fine as
she remembered it. But then she had been younger
when she had had so much fun there.

The knowledge or conviction about the party for Doc
was no sudden thing. It did not burst out full blown.
People knew about it but let it grow gradually like a
pupa in the cocoons of their imaginations.

Mack was realistic about it. "Last time we forced
her," he told the boys. "You can't never give a good
party that way. You got to let her creep up on you."

"Well when's it going to be?" Jones asked
impatiently.

"I don't know," said Mack.

"Is it gonna be a surprise party?" Hazel asked.

"It ought to, that's the best kind," said Mack.

Darling brought him a tennis ball she had found and
he threw it out the door into the weeds. She bounced
away after it.

Hazel said, "If we knew when was Doc's birthday,
we could give him a birthday party."

Mack's mouth was open. Hazel constantly surprised him. "By God, Hazel, you got something," he cried. "Yes, sir, if it was his birthday there'd be presents. That's just the thing. All we got to find out is when it is."

"That ought to be easy," said Hughie. "Why don't we ask him?"

"Hell," said Mack. "Then he'd catch on. You ask a guy when is his birthday and especially if you've already give him a party like we done, and he'll know what you want to know for. Maybe I'll just go over and smell around a little and not let on."

"I'll go with you," said Hazel.

"No—if two of us went, he might figure we were up to something."

"Well, hell, it was my idear," said Hazel.

"I know," said Mack. "And when it comes off why I'll tell Doc it was your idear. But I think I better go over alone."

"How is he—friendly?" Eddie asked.

"Sure, he's all right."

Mack found Doc way back in the downstairs part of the laboratory. He was dressed in a long rubber apron and he wore rubber gloves to protect his hands from the formaldehyde. He was injecting the veins and arteries of small dogfish with color mass. His little ball mill rolled over and over, mixing the blue mass. The red fluid was already in the pressure gun. Doc's fine hands worked precisely, slipping the needle into place and pressing the compressed air trigger that forced the color into the veins. He laid the finished fish in a neat pile. He would have to go over these again to put blue mass in the arteries. The dogfish made good dissection specimens.

"Hi, Doc," said Mack. "Keepin' pretty busy?"

"Busy as I want," said Doc. "How's the pup?"

"Doin' just fine. She would of died if it hadn't been for you."

For a moment a wave of caution went over Doc and then slipped off. Ordinarily a compliment made him wary. He had been dealing with Mack for a long time. But the tone had nothing but gratefulness in it. He knew how Mack felt about the pup. "How are things going up at the Palace?"

"Fine, Doc, just fine. We got two new chairs. I wish you'd come up and see us. It's pretty nice up there now."

"I will," said Doc. "Eddie still bring back the jug?"

"Sure," said Mack. "He ain't putting' beer in it no more and I think the stuff is better. It's got more zip."

"It had plenty of zip before," said Doc.

Mack waited patiently. Sooner or later Doc was going to wade into it and he was waiting. If Doc seemed to open the subject himself it would be less suspicious. This was always Mack's method.

"Haven't seen Hazel for some time. He isn't sick, is he?"

"No," said Mack and he opened the campaign. "Hazel is all right. Him and Hughie are havin' one hell of a battle. Been goin' on for a week," he chuckled. "An' the funny thing is it's about somethin' they don't neither of them know nothin' about. I stayed out of it because I don't know nothin' about it neither, but not them. They've even got a little mad at each other."

"What's it about?" Doc asked.

"Well, sir," said Mack, "Hazel's all the time buyin' these here charts and lookin' up lucky days and stars and stuff like that. And Hughie says it's all a bunch of ma-larkey. Hughie, he says if you know when a guy is born you can tell about him and Hughie says they're just sel-lin' Hazel them charts for two bits apiece. Me, I don't know nothin' about it. What do you think, Doc?"

"I'd kind of side with Hughie," said Doc. He stopped the ball mill, washed out the color gun and filled it with blue mass.

"They got goin' hot the other night," said Mack. "They ask me when I'm born so I tell 'em April 12 and Hazel he goes and buys one of them charts and read all about me. Well it did seem to hit in some places. But it was nearly all good stuff and a guy will believe good stuff about himself. It said I'm brave and smart and kind to my friends. But Hazel says it's all true. When's your birthday, Doc?" At the end of the long discussion it sounded perfectly casual. You couldn't put your finger on it. But it must be remembered that Doc had known Mack a very long time. If he had not he would have said December 18 which was his birth-day instead of October 27 which was not. "October 27," said Doc. "Ask Hazel what that makes me."

"It's probably so much malarkey," said Mack, "but Hazel he takes it serious. I'll ask him to look you up, Doc."

When Mack left, Doc wondered casually what the build-up was. For he had recognized it as a lead. He knew Mack's technique, his method. He recognized his style. And he wondered to what purpose Mack could put the information. It was only later when ru-mors began to creep in that Doc added the whole thing up. Now he felt slightly relieved, for he had expected Mack to put the bite on him.

26

The two boys played in the boat works yard until a cat climbed the fence. Instantly they gave chase, drove it across the tracks and there filled their pockets with granite stones from the roadbed. The cat got away from them in the tall weeds but they kept the stones because they were perfect in weight, shape, and size for throwing. You can't ever tell when you're going to need a stone like that. They turned down Cannery Row and whanged a stone at the corrugated iron front of Morden's Cannery. A startled man looked out the office window and then rushed for the door, but the boys were too quick for him. They were lying behind a wooden stringer in the lot before he even got near the door. He couldn't have found them in a hundred years.

"I bet he could look all his life and he couldn't find us," said Joey.

They got tired of hiding after a while with no one looking for them. They got up and strolled on down Cannery Row. They looked a long time in Lee's window coveting the pliers, the hack saws, the engineers' caps and the bananas. Then they crossed the street and sat down on the lower step of the stairs that went to the second story of the laboratory.

Joey said, "You know, this guy in here got babies in bottles."

"What kind of babies?" Willard asked.

"Regular babies, only before they're borned."

"I don't believe it," said Willard.

"Well, it's true. The Sprague kid seen them and he says they ain't no bigger than this and they got little hands and feet and eyes."

"And hair?" Willard demanded.

"Well, the Sprague kid didn't say about hair."

"You should of asked him. I think he's a liar."

"You better not let him hear you say that," said Joey.

"Well, you can tell him I said it. I ain't afraid of him and I ain't afraid of you. I ain't afraid of anybody. You want to make something of it?" Joey didn't answer. "Well, do you?"

"No," said Joey. "I was thinkin', why don't we just go up and ask the guy if he's got babies in bottles? Maybe he'd show them to us, that is if he's got any."

"He ain't here," said Willard. "When he's here, his car's here. He's away some place. I think it's a lie. I think the Sprague kid is a liar. I think you're a liar. You want to make something of that?"

It was a lazy day. Willard was going to have to work hard to get up any excitement. "I think you're a coward, too. You want to make something of that?" Joey didn't answer. Willard changed his tactics. "Where's your old man now?" he asked in a conversational tone.

"He's dead," said Joey.

"Oh yeah? I didn't hear. What'd he die of?"

For a moment Joey was silent. He knew Willard knew but he couldn't let on he knew, not without fighting Willard, and Joey was afraid of Willard.

"He committed—he killed himself."

"Yeah?" Willard put on a long face. "How'd he do it?"

"He took rat poison."

Willard's voice shrieked with laughter. "What'd he think—he was a rat?"

Joey chuckled a little at the joke, just enough, that is.

"He must of thought he was a rat," Willard cried. "Did he go crawling around like this—look, Joey— like this? Did he wrinkle up his nose like this? Did he have a big old long tail?" Willard was helpless with laughter. "Why'n't he just get a rat trap and put his head in it?" They laughed themselves out on that one, Willard really wore it out. Then he probed for another joke. "What'd he look like when he took it—like this?" He crossed his eyes and opened his mouth and stuck out his tongue.

"He was sick all day," said Joey. "He didn't die 'til the middle of the night. It hurt him."

Willard said, "What'd he do it for?"

"He couldn't get a job," said Joey. "Nearly a year he couldn't get a job. And you know the funny thing? The next morning a guy come around to give him a job."

Willard tried to recapture his joke. "I guess he just figured he was a rat," he said, but it fell through even for Willard.

Joey stood up and put his hands in his pockets. He saw a little coppery shine in the gutter and walked toward it but just as he reached it Willard shoved him aside and picked up the penny.

"I saw it first," Joey cried. "It's mine."

"You want to try and make something of it?" said Willard. "Why'n't you go take some rat poison?"

27

Mack and the boys—the Virtues, the Beatitudes, the Beauties. They sat in the Palace Flophouse and they were the stone dropped in the pool, the impulse which sent out ripples to all of Cannery Row and beyond, to Pacific Grove, to Monterey, even over the hill to Carmel.

"This time," said Mack, "we got to be sure he gets to the party. If he don't get there, we don't give it."

"Where we going to give it this time?" Jones asked.

Mack tipped his chair back against the wall and hooked his feet around the front legs. "I've give that a lot of thought," he said. "Of course we could give it here but it would be pretty hard to surprise him here. And Doc likes his own place. He's got his music there." Mack scowled around the room. "I don't know who broke his phonograph last time," he said. "But if anybody so much as lays a finger on it next time I personally will kick the hell out of him."

"I guess we'll just have to give it at his place," said Hughie.

People didn't get the news of the party—the knowledge of it just slowly grew up in them. And no one was invited. Everyone was going. October 27 had a mental red circle around it. And since it was to be a birthday party there were presents to be considered.

Take the girls at Dora's. All of them had at one time or another gone over to the laboratory for advice or medicine or simply for unprofessional company. And they had seen Doc's bed. It was covered with an old faded red blanket full of fox tails and burrs and sand, for he took it on all his collecting trips. If money came in he bought laboratory equipment. It never occurred to him to buy a new blanket for himself. Dora's girls were making him a patchwork quilt, a beautiful thing of silk. And since most of the silk available came from underclothing and evening dresses, the quilt was glorious in strips of flesh pink and orchid and pale yellow and cerise. They worked on it in the late mornings and in the afternoons before the boys from the sardine fleet came in. Under the community of effort, those fights and ill feelings that always are present in a whore house completely disappeared.

Lee Chong got out and inspected a twenty-five-foot string of firecrackers and a big bag of China lily bulbs. These to his way of thinking were the finest things you could have for a party.

Sam Malloy had long had a theory of antiques. He knew that old furniture and glass and crockery, which had not been very valuable in its day, had when time went by taken on desirability and cash value out of all proportion to its beauty or utility. He knew of one chair that had brought five hundred dollars. Sam collected pieces of historic automobiles and he was convinced that some day his collection, after making him very rich, would repose on black velvet in the best museums. Sam gave the party a good deal of thought and then he went over his treasures which he kept in a big locked box behind the boiler. He decided to give Doc one of his finest pieces—the connecting rod and piston from a 1916 Chalmers. He rubbed and polished this beauty until it gleamed like a piece of ancient armor. He made a little box for it and lined it with black cloth.

Mack and the boys gave the problem considerable thought and came to the conclusion that Doc always wanted cats and had some trouble getting them. Mack brought out his double cage. They borrowed a female in an interesting condition and set their trap under the cypress tree at the top of the vacant lot. In the corner of the Palace they built a wire cage and in it their collection of angry tom cats grew with every night. Jones had to make two trips a day to the canneries for fish heads to feed their charges. Mack considered and correctly that twenty-five tom cats would be as nice a present as they could give Doc.

"No decorations this time," said Mack. "Just a good solid party with lots of liquor."

Gay heard about the party clear over in the Salinas jail and he made a deal with the sheriff to get off that night and borrowed two dollars from him for a round trip bus ticket. Gay had been very nice to the sheriff who wasn't a man to forget it, particularly because election was coming up and Gay could, or said he could, swing quite a few votes. Besides, Gay could give the Salinas jail a bad name if he wanted to.

Henri had suddenly decided that the old-fashioned pincushion was an art form which had flowered and reached its peak in the Nineties and had since been neglected. He revived the form and was delighted to see what could be done with colored pins. The picture was never completed—you could change it by rearranging the pins. He was preparing a group of these pieces for a one-man show when he heard about the party and he instantly abandoned his own work and began a giant pincushion for Doc. It was to be an intricate and provocative design in green, yellow, and blue pins, all cool colors, and its title was Pre-Cambrian Memory.

Henri's friend Eric, a learned barber who collected the first editions of writers who never had a second edition or a second book, decided to give Doc a rowing machine he had got at the bankruptcy proceedings of a client with a three-year barber bill. The rowing machine was in fine condition. No one had rowed it much. No one ever uses a rowing machine.

The conspiracy grew and there were endless visits back and forth, discussion of presents, of liquor, of what time will we start and nobody must tell Doc.

Doc didn't know when he first became aware that something was going on that concerned him. In Lee Chong's, conversation stopped when he entered. At first it seemed to him that people were cold to him. When at least half a dozen people asked him what he was doing October 27 he was puzzled, for he had forgotten he had given this date as his birthday. Actually he had been interested in the horoscope for a spurious birth date but Mack had never mentioned it again and so Doc forgot it.

One evening he stopped in at the Halfway House because they had a draft beer he liked and kept it at the right temperature. He gulped his first glass and then settled down to enjoy his second when he heard a drunk talking to the bartender. "You goin' to the party?"

"What party?"

"Well," said the drunk confidentially, "you know Doc, down in Cannery Row."

The bartender looked up the bar and then back.

"Well," said the drunk, "they're givin' him a hell of a party on his birthday."

"Who is?"

"Everybody."

Doc mulled this over. He did not know the drunk at all.

His reaction to the idea was not simple. He felt a great warmth that they should want to give him a party and at the same time he quaked inwardly remembering the last one they had given.

Now everything fell into place—Mack's question and the silences when he was about. He thought of it a lot that night sitting beside his desk. He glanced about considering what things would have to be locked up. He knew the party was going to cost him plenty.

The next day he began making his own preparations for the party. His best records he carried into the back room where they could be locked away. He moved every bit of equipment that was breakable back there too. He knew how it would be—his guests would be hungry and they wouldn't bring anything to eat. They would run out of liquor early, they always did. A little wearily he went up to the Thrift Market where there was a fine and understanding butcher. They discussed meat for some time. Doc ordered fifteen pounds of steaks, ten pounds of tomatoes, twelve heads of let-

tuce, six loaves of bread, a big jar of peanut butter and
one of strawberry jam, five gallons of wine and four
quarts of a good substantial but not distinguished
whiskey. He knew he would have trouble at the bank
the first of the month. Three or four such parties, he
thought, and he would lose the laboratory.

Meanwhile on the Row the planning reached a cre-
scendo. Doc was right, no one thought of food but
there were odd pints and quarts put away all over. The
collection of presents was growing and the guest list, if
there had been one, was a little like a census. At the
Bear Flag a constant discussion went on about what to
wear. Since they would not be working, the girls did
not want to wear the long beautiful dresses which were
their uniforms. They decided to wear street clothes. It
wasn't as simple as it sounded. Dora insisted that a
skeleton crew remain on duty to take care of the regulars. The girls divided up into shifts, some to stay until
they were relieved by others. They had to flip for who
would go to the party first. The first ones would see
Doc's face when they gave him the beautiful quilt.
They had it on a frame in the dining room and it was
nearly finished. Mrs. Malloy had put aside her bedspread for a while. She was crocheting six doilies for
Doc's beer glasses. The first excitement was gone from
the Row now and its place was taken by a deadly
cumulative earnestness. There were fifteen tom cats in
the cage at the Palace Flophouse and their yowling
made Darling a little nervous at night.

28

Sooner or later Frankie was bound to hear about the party. For Frankie drifted about like a small cloud. He was always on the edge of groups. No one noticed him or paid any attention to him. You couldn't tell whether he was listening or not. But Frankie did hear about the party and he heard about the presents and a feeling of fullness swelled in him and a feeling of sick longing.

In the window of Jacob's Jewelry Store was the most beautiful thing in the world. It had been there a long time. It was a black onyx clock with a gold face but on top of it was the real beauty. On top was a bronze group—St. George killing the dragon. The dragon was on his back with his claws in the air and in his breast was St. George's spear. The Saint was in full armor with the visor raised and he rode a fat, big-buttocked horse. With his spear he pinned the dragon to the ground. But the wonderful thing was that he wore a pointed beard and he looked a little like Doc.

Frankie walked to Alvarado Street several times a week to stand in front of the window and look at this beauty. He dreamed about it too, dreamed of running his fingers over the rich, smooth bronze. He had known about it for months when he heard of the party and the presents.

Frankie stood on the sidewalk for an hour before he went inside. "Well?" said Mr. Jacobs. He had given Frankie a visual frisk as he came in and he knew there wasn't 75 cents on him.

"How much is that?" Frankie asked huskily.

"What?"

"That."

"You mean the clock? Fifty dollars—with thé group seventy-five dollars."

Frankie walked out without replying. He went down to the beach and crawled under an overturned rowboat and peeked out at the little waves. The bronze beauty was so strong in his head that it seemed to stand out in front of him. And a frantic trapped feeling came over him. He had to get the beauty. His eyes were fierce when he thought of it.

He stayed under the boat all day and at night he emerged and went back to Alvarado Street. While people went to the movies and came out and went to the Golden Poppy, he walked up and down the block. And he didn't get tired or sleepy, for the beauty burned in him like fire.

At last the people thinned out and gradually disappeared from the streets and the parked cars drove away and the town settled to sleep.

A policeman looked closely at Frankie. "What you doing out?" he asked.

Frankie took to his heels and fled around the corner and hid behind a barrel in the alley. At two-thirty he crept to the door of Jacob's and tried the knob. It was locked. Frankie went back to the alley and sat behind the barrel and thought. He saw a broken piece of concrete lying beside the barrel and picked it up.

The policeman reported that he heard the crash and ran to it. Jacob's window was broken. He saw the prisoner walking rapidly away and chased him. He didn't know how the boy could run that far and that fast carrying fifty pounds of clock and bronze, but the prisoner nearly got away. If he had not blundered into a blind street he would have got away.

The chief called Doc the next day. "Come on down, will you? I want to talk to you."

They brought Frankie in very dirty and frowzy. His eyes were red but he held his mouth firm and he even smiled a little welcome when he saw Doc.

"What's the matter, Frankie?" Doc asked.

"He broke into Jacob's last night," the chief said. "Stole some stuff. We got in touch with his mother. She says it's not her fault because he hangs around your place all the time."

"Frankie—you shouldn't have done it," said Doc. The heavy stone of inevitability was on his heart. "Can't you parole him to me?" Doc asked.

"I don't think the judge will do it," said the chief. "We've got a mental report. You know what's wrong with him?"

"Yes," said Doc, "I know."

"And you know what's likely to happen when he comes into puberty?"

"Yes," said Doc, "I know," and the stone weighed terribly on his heart.

"The doctor thinks we better put him away. We

couldn't before, but now he's got a felony on him, I think we better."

As Frankie listened the welcome died in his eyes.

"What did he take?" Doc asked.

"A great big clock and a bronze statue."

"I'll pay for it."

"Oh, we got it back. I don't think the judge will hear of it. It'll just happen again. You know that."

"Yes," said Doc softly, "I know. But maybe he had a reason. Frankie," he said, "why did you take it?"

Frankie looked a long time at him. "I love you," he said.

Doc ran out and got in his car and went collecting in the caves below Pt. Lobos.

29

At four o'clock on October 27 Doc finished bottling the last of a lot of jellyfish. He washed out the formaline jug, cleaned his forceps, powdered and took off his rubber gloves. He went upstairs, fed the rats, and put some of his best records and his microscopes in the back room. Then he locked it. Sometimes an illuminated guest wanted to play with the rattlesnakes. By making careful preparations, by foreseeing possibilities, Doc hoped to make this party as non-lethal as possible without making it dull.

He put on a pot of coffee, started the *Great Fugue* on the phonograph, and took a shower. He was very quick about it, for he was dressed in clean clothes and was having his cup of coffee before the music was completed.

He looked out through the window at the lot and up at the Palace but no one was moving. Doc didn't know who or how many were coming to his party. But he knew he was watched. He had been conscious of it all day. Not that he had seen anyone, but someone or several people had kept him in sight. So it was to be a

surprise party. He might as well be surprised. He
would follow his usual routine as though nothing were
happening. He crossed to Lee Chong's and bought two
quarts of beer. There seemed to be a suppressed Oriental excitement at Lee's. So they were coming too.
Doc went back to the laboratory and poured out a glass
of beer. He drank the first off for thirst and poured a
second one for taste. The lot and the street were still
deserted.

Mack and the boys were in the Palace and the door
was closed. All afternoon the stove had roared, heating
water for baths. Even Darling had been bathed and
she wore a red bow around her neck.

"What time you think we should go over?" Hazel
asked.

"I don't think before eight o'clock," said Mack.
"But I don't see nothin' against us havin' a short one to
kind of get warmed up."

"How about Doc getting warmed up?" Hughie said.
"Maybe I ought to just take him a bottle like it was
just nothing."

"No," said Mack. "Doc just went over to Lee's for
some beer."

'You think he suspects anything?" Jones asked.

"How could he?" asked Mack.

In the corner cage two tom cats started an argument
and the whole cageful commented with growls and
arched backs. There were only twenty-one cats. They
had fallen short of their mark.

"I wonder how we'll get them cats over there?" Hazel began. "We can't carry that big cage through the
door."

"We won't," said Mack. "Remember how it was

with the frogs. No, we'll just tell Doc about them. He
can come over and get them." Mack got up and
opened one of Eddie's wining jugs. "We might as well
get warmed up," he said.

At five-thirty the old Chinaman flap-flapped down
the hill, past the Palace. He crossed the lot, crossed
the street, and disappeared between Western Biological and the Hediondo.

At the Bear Flag the girls were getting ready. A
kind of anchor watch had been chosen by straws. The
ones who stayed were to be relieved every hour.

Dora was splendid. Her hair freshly dyed orange
was curled and piled on her head. She wore her wedding ring and a big diamond brooch on her breast. Her
dress was white silk with a black bamboo pattern. In
the bedrooms the reverse of ordinary procedure was in
practice.

Those who were staying wore long evening dresses
while those who were going had on short print dresses
and looked very pretty. The quilt, finished and
backed, was in a big cardboard box in the bar. The
bouncer grumbled a little, for it had been decided that
he couldn't go to the party. Someone had to look after
the house. Contrary to orders, each girl had a pint
hidden and each girl watched for the signal to fortify
herself a little for the party.

Dora strode magnificently into her office and closed
the door. She unlocked the top drawer of the rolltop
desk, took out a bottle and a glass and poured herself
a snort. And the bottle clinked softly on the glass. A
girl listening outside the door heard the clink and
spread the word. Dora would not be able to smell
breaths now. And the girls rushed for their rooms and

got out their pints. Dusk had come to Cannery Row, the gray time between daylight and street light. Phyllis Mae peeked around the curtain in the front parlor.

"Can you see him?" Doris asked.

"Yeah. He's got the lights on. He's sitting there like he's reading. Jesus, how that guy does read. You'd think he'd ruin his eyes. He's got a glass of beer in his hand."

"Well," said Doris, "we might as well have a little one, I guess."

Phyllis Mae was still limping a little but she was as good as new. She could, she said, lick her weight in City Councilmen. "Seems kind of funny," she said. "There he is, sitting over there and he don't know what's going to happen."

"He never comes in here for a trick," Doris said a little sadly.

"Lots of guys don't want to pay," said Phyllis Mae. "Costs them more but they figure it different."

"Well, hell, maybe he likes them."

"Likes who?"

"Them girls that go over there."

"Oh, yeah—maybe he does. I been over there. He never made a pass at me."

"He wouldn't," said Doris. "But that don't mean if you didn't work here you wouldn't have to fight your way out."

"You mean he don't like our profession?"

"No, I don't mean that at all. He probably figures a girl that's workin' has got a different attitude."

They had another small snort.

In her office Dora poured herself one more, swallowed it and locked the drawer again. She fixed her perfect hair in the wall mirror, inspected her shining red nails, and went out to the bar. Alfred the bouncer was sulking. It wasn't anything he said nor was his expression unpleasant, but he was sulking just the same. Dora looked him over coldly. "I guess you figure you're getting the blocks, don't you?"

"No," said Alfred. "No, it's quite all right."

That quite threw Dora. "Quite all right, is it? You got a job, Mister. Do you want to keep it or not?"

"It's quite all right," Alfred said frostily. "I ain't putting out no beef." He put his elbows on the bar and studied himself in the mirror. "You just go and enjoy yourself," he said. "I'll take care of everything here. You don't need to worry."

Dora melted under his pain. "Look," she said. "I don't like to have the place without a man. Some lush might get smart and the kids couldn't handle him. But a little later you can come over and you could kind of keep your eye on the place out the window. How would that be? You could see if anything happened."

"Well," said Alfred, "I would like to come." He was mollified by her permission. "Later I might drop over for just a minute or two. They was a mean drunk in last night. An' I don't know, Dora—I kind of lost my nerve since I bust that guy's back. I just ain't sure of myself no more. I'm gonna pull a punch some night and get took."

"You need a rest," said Dora. "Maybe I'll get Mack to fill in and you can take a couple of weeks off." She was a wonderful madam, Dora was.

Over at the laboratory, Doc had a little whiskey after his beer. He was feeling a little mellow. It seemed a nice thing to him that they would give him a party. He played the *Pavane to a Dead Princess* and felt sentimental and a little sad. And because of his feeling he went on with *Daphnis and Chloe*. There was a passage in it that reminded him of something else. The observers in Athens before Marathon reported seeing a great line of dust crossing the Plain, and they heard the clash of arms and they heard the Eleusinian Chant. There was part of the music that reminded him of that picture.

When it was done he got another whiskey and he debated in his mind about the *Brandenburg*. That would snap him out of the sweet and sickly mood he was getting into. But what was wrong with the sweet and sickly mood? It was rather pleasant. "I can play anything I want," he said aloud. "I can play *Clair de Lune* or *The Maiden with Flaxen Hair*. I'm a free man."

He poured a whiskey and drank it. And he compromised with the *Moonlight Sonata*. He could see the neon light of La Ida blinking on and off. And then the street light in front of the Bear Flag came on.

A squadron of huge brown beetles hurled themselves against the light and then fell to the ground and moved their legs and felt around with their antennae. A lady cat strolled lonesomely along the gutter looking for adventure. She wondered what had happened to all the tom cats who had made life interesting and the nights hideous.

Mr. Malloy on his hands and knees peered out of the boiler door to see if anyone had gone to the party yet. In the Palace the boys sat restlessly watching the black hands of the alarm clock.

30

The nature of parties has been imperfectly studied. It is, however, generally understood that a party has a pathology, that it is a kind of an individual and that it is likely to be a very perverse individual. And it is also generally understood that a party hardly ever goes the way it is planned or intended. This last, of course, excludes those dismal slave parties, whipped and controlled and dominated, given by ogreish professional hostesses. These are not parties at all but acts and demonstrations, about as spontaneous as peristalsis and as interesting as its end product.

Probably everyone in Cannery Row had projected his imagination to how the party would be—the shouts of greeting, the congratulation, the noise and good feeling. And it didn't start that way at all. Promptly at eight o'clock Mack and the boys, combed and clean, picked up their jugs and marched down the chicken walk, over the railroad track, through the lot across the street and up the steps of Western Biological. Everyone was embarrassed. Doc held the door open

and Mack made a little speech. "Being as how it's
your birthday, I and the boys thought we would wish
you happy birthday and we got twenty-one cats for you
for a present."

He stopped and they stood forlornly on the stairs.

"Come on in," said Doc. "Why—I'm—I'm surprised. I didn't even know you knew it was my birthday."

"All tom cats," said Hazel. "We didn't bring 'em
down."

They sat down formally in the room at the left.
There was a long silence. "Well," said Doc, "now
you're here, how about a little drink?"

Mack said, "We brought a little snort," and he indicated the three jugs Eddie had been accumulating.
"They ain't no beer in it," said Eddie.

Doc covered his early evening reluctance. "No," he
said. "You've got to have a drink with me. It just
happens I laid in some whiskey."

They were just seated formally, sipping delicately at
the whiskey, when Dora and the girls came in. They
presented the quilt. Doc laid it over his bed and it was
beautiful. And they accepted a little drink. Mr. and
Mrs. Malloy followed with their presents.

"Lots of folks don't know what this stuff's going to
be worth," said Sam Malloy as he brought out the
Chalmers 1916 piston and connecting rod. "There
probably isn't three of these here left in the world."

And now people began to arrive in droves. Henri
came in with a pincushion three by four feet. He
wanted to give a lecture on his new art form but by this
time the formality was broken. Mr. and Mrs. Gay came
in. Lee Chong presented the great string of firecrack-

ers and the China lily bulbs. Someone ate the lily
bulbs by eleven o'clock but the firecrackers lasted
longer. A group of comparative strangers came in from
La Ida. The stiffness was going out of the party
quickly. Dora sat in a kind of throne, her orange hair
flaming. She held her whiskey glass daintily with her
little finger extended. And she kept an eye on the girls
to see that they conducted themselves properly. Doc
put dance music on the phonograph and he went to the
kitchen and began to fry the steaks.

The first fight was not a bad one. One of the group
from La Ida made an immoral proposal to one of Dora's
girls. She protested and Mack and the boys, outraged
at this breach of propriety, threw him out quickly and
without breaking anything. They felt good then, for
they knew they were contributing.

Out in the kitchen Doc was frying steaks in three
skillets, and he cut up tomatoes and piled up sliced
bread. He felt very good. Mack was personally taking
care of the phonograph. He had found an album of
Benny Goodman's trios. Dancing had started, indeed
the party was beginning to take on depth and vigor.
Eddie went into the office and did a tap dance. Doc
had taken a pint with him to the kitchen and he helped
himself from the bottle. He was feeling better and
better. Everybody was surprised when he served the
meat. Nobody was really hungry and they cleaned it
up instantly. Now the food set the party into a kind of
rich digestive sadness. The whiskey was gone and Doc
brought out the gallons of wine.

Dora, sitting enthroned, said, "Doc, play some of
that nice music. I get Christ awful sick of that juke
box over home."

Then Doc played *Ardo* and the *Amor* from an album of Monteverdi. And the guests sat quietly and their eyes were inward. Dora breathed beauty. Two newcomers crept up the stairs and entered quietly. Doc was feeling a golden pleasant sadness. The guests were silent when the music stopped. Doc brought out a book and he read in a clear, deep voice:

Even now
If I see in my soul the citron-breasted fair one
Still gold-tinted, her face like our night stars,
Drawing unto her; her body beaten about with
    flame,
Wounded by the flaring spear of love,
My first of all by reason of her fresh years,
Then is my heart buried alive in snow.

Even now
If my girl with lotus eyes came to me again
Weary with the dear weight of young love,
Again I would give her to these starved twins of
    arms
And from her mouth drink down the heavy wine,
As a reeling pirate bee in fluttered ease
Steals up the honey from the nenuphar.

Even now
If I saw her lying all wide eyes
And with collyrium the indent of her cheek
Lengthened to the bright ear and her pale side
So suffering the fever of my distance,
Then would my love for her be ropes of flowers,
    and night
A black-haired lover on the breasts of day.

Even now
My eyes that hurry to see no more are painting,
    painting
Faces of my lost girl. O golden rings
That tap against cheeks of small magnolia leaves,
O whitest so soft parchment where
My poor divorcèd lips have written excellent
Stanzas of kisses, and will write no more.

Even now
Death sends me the flickering of powdery lids
Over wild eyes and the pity of her slim body
All broken up with the weariness of joy;
The little red flowers of her breasts to be my
    comfort
Moving above scarves, and for my sorrow
Wet crimson lips that once I marked as mine.

Even now
They chatter her weakness through the two bazaars
Who was so strong to love me. And small men
That buy and sell for silver being slaves
Crinkle the fat about their eyes; and yet
No Prince of the Cities of the Sea has taken her,
Leading to his grim bed. Little lonely one,
You clung to me as a garment clings; my girl.

Even now
I love long black eyes that caress like silk,
Ever and ever sad and laughing eyes,
Whose lids make such sweet shadow when they
    close
It seems another beautiful look of hers.

I love a fresh mouth, ah, a scented mouth,
And curving hair, subtle as a smoke,
And light fingers, and laughter of green gems.

Even now
I remember that you made answer very softly,
We being one soul, your hand on my hair,
The burning memory rounding your near lips:
I have seen the priestesses of Rati make love at
    moon fall
And then in a carpeted hall with a bright gold
    lamp
Lie down carelessly anywhere to sleep.[1]

Phyllis Mae was openly weeping when he stopped
and Dora herself dabbed at her eyes. Hazel was so
taken by the sound of the words that he had not listened to their meaning. But a little world-sadness had
slipped over all of them. Everyone was remembering a
lost love, everyone a call.

Mack said, "Jesus, that's pretty. Reminds me of a
dame——" and he let it pass. They filled the wine
glasses and became quiet. The party was slipping
away in sweet sadness. Eddie went out in the office
and did a little tap dance and came back and sat down
again. The party was about to recline and go to sleep
when there was a tramp of feet on the stairs. A great
voice shouted, "Where's the girls?"

Mack got up almost happily and crossed quickly to
the door. And a smile of joy illuminated the faces of
Hughie and Jones. "What girls you got in mind?"
Mack asked softly.

[1] "Black Marigolds," translated from the Sanskrit by E. Powys Mathers.

"Ain't this a whore house? Cab driver said they was one down here."

"You made a mistake, Mister." Mack's voice was gay.

"Well, what's them dames in there?"

They joined battle then. They were the crew of a San Pedro tuna boat, good hard happy fight-wise men. With the first rush they burst through to the party. Dora's girls had each one slipped off a shoe and held it by the toe. As the fight raged by they would clip a man on the head with the spike heel. Dora leaped for the kitchen and came roaring out with a meat grinder. Even Doc was happy. He flailed about with the Chalmers 1916 piston and connecting rod.

It was a good fight. Hazel tripped and got kicked in the face twice before he could get to his feet again. The Franklin stove went over with a crash. Driven to a corner the newcomers defended themselves with heavy books from the bookcases. But gradually they were driven back. The two front windows were broken out. Suddenly Alfred, who had heard the trouble from across the street, attacked from the rear with his favorite weapon, an indoor ball bat. The fight raged down the steps and into the street and across the lot. The front door was hanging limply from one hinge again. Doc's shirt was torn off and his slight strong shoulder dripped blood from a scratch. The enemy was driven half-way up the lot when sirens sounded. Doc's birthday party had barely time to get inside the laboratory and wedge the broken door closed and turn out the lights before the police car cruised up. The cops didn't find anything. But the party was sitting in the dark giggling happily and drinking wine. The shift changed

at the Bear Flag. The fresh contingent raged in full of
hell. And then the party really got going. The cops
came back, looked in, clicked their tongues and
joined it. Mack and the boys used the squad car to go
to Jimmy Brucia's for more wine and Jimmy came back
with them. You could hear the roar of the party from
end to end of Cannery Row. The party had all the best
qualities of a riot and a night on the barricades. The
crew from the San Pedro tuna boat crept humbly back
and joined the party. They were embraced and ad-
mired. A woman five blocks away called the police to
complain about the noise and couldn't get anyone. The
cops reported their own car stolen and found it later on
the beach. Doc sitting cross-legged on the table smiled
and tapped his fingers gently on his knee. Mack and
Phyllis Mae were doing Indian wrestling on the floor.
And the cool bay wind blew in through the broken
windows. It was then that someone lighted the twenty-
five-foot string of firecrackers.

31

A well-grown gopher took up residence in a thicket of mallow weeds in the vacant lot on Cannery Row. It was a perfect place. The deep green luscious mallows towered up crisp and rich and as they matured their little cheeses hung down provocatively. The earth was perfect for a gopher hole too, black and soft and yet with a little clay in it so that it didn't crumble and the tunnels didn't cave in. The gopher was fat and sleek and he had always plenty of food in his cheek pouches. His little ears were clean and well set and his eyes were as black as old-fashioned pin heads and just about the same size. His digging hands were strong and the fur on his back was glossy brown and the fawn-colored fur on his chest was incredibly soft and rich. He had long curving yellow teeth and a little short tail. Altogether he was a beautiful gopher and in the prime of his life.

He came to the place over land and found it good and he began his burrow on a little eminence where he could look out among the mallow weeds and see the trucks go by on Cannery Row. He could watch the feet of Mack and the boys as they crossed the lot to the Palace Flophouse. As he dug down into the coal-black earth he found it even more perfect, for there were great rocks under the soil. When he made his great chamber for the storing of food it was under a rock so that it could never cave in no matter how hard it rained. It was a place where he could settle down and raise any number of families and the burrow could increase in all directions.

It was beautiful in the early morning when he first poked his head out of the burrow. The mallows filtered green light down on him and the first rays of the rising sun shone into his hole and warmed it so that he lay there content and very comfortable.

When he had dug his great chamber and his four emergency exits and his waterproof deluge room, the gopher began to store food. He cut down only the perfect mallow stems and trimmed them to the exact length he needed and he took them down the hole and stacked them neatly in his great chamber, and arranged them so they wouldn't ferment or get sour. He had found the perfect place to live. There were no gardens about so no one would think of setting a trap for him. Cats there were, many of them, but they were so bloated with fish heads and guts from the canneries that they had long ago given up hunting. The soil was sandy enough so that water never stood about or filled a hole for long. The gopher worked and worked until he had his great chamber crammed with food. Then he made little side chambers for the babies who would inhabit them. In a few years there might be thousands of his progeny spreading out from this original hearthstone.

But as time went on the gopher began to be a little

impatient, for no female appeared. He sat in the entrance of his hole in the morning and made penetrating
squeaks that are inaudible to the human ear but can
be heard deep in the earth by other gophers. And still
no female appeared. Finally in a sweat of impatience
he went up across the track until he found another
gopher hole. He squeaked provocatively in the entrance. He heard a rustling and smelled female and
then out of the hole came an old battle-torn bull
gopher who mauled and bit him so badly that he crept
home and lay in his great chamber for three days
recovering and he lost two toes from one front paw
from that fight.

Again he waited and squeaked beside his beautiful
burrow in the beautiful place but no female ever came
and after a while he had to move away. He had to
move two blocks up the hill to a dahlia garden where
they put out traps every night.

32

Doc awakened very slowly and clumsily like a fat man getting out of a swimming pool. His mind broke the surface and fell back several times. There was red lipstick on his beard. He opened one eye, saw the brilliant colors of the quilt and closed his eye quickly. But after a while he looked again. His eye went past the quilt to the floor, to the broken plate in the corner, to the glasses standing on the table turned over on the floor, to the spilled wine and the books like heavy fallen butterflies. There were little bits of curled red paper all over the place and the sharp smell of firecrackers. He could see through the kitchen door to the steak plates stacked high and the skillets deep in grease. Hundreds of cigarette butts were stamped out on the floor. And under the firecracker smell was a fine combination of wine and whiskey and perfume. His eye stopped for a moment on a little pile of hairpins in the middle of the floor.

He rolled over slowly and supporting himself on one elbow he looked out the broken window. Cannery Row was quiet and sunny. The boiler door was open. The door of the Palace Flophouse was closed. A man slept peacefully among the weeds in the vacant lot. The Bear Flag was shut up tight.

Doc got up and went into the kitchen and lighted the gas water heater on his way to the toilet. Then he came back and sat on the edge of the bed and worked his toes together while he surveyed the wreckage. From up the hill he could hear the church bells ringing. When the gas heater began rumbling he went back to the bathroom and took a shower and he put on blue jeans and a flannel shirt. Lee Chong was closed but he saw who was at the door and opened it. He went to the refrigerator and brought out a quart of beer without being asked. Doc paid him.

"Good time?" Lee asked. His brown eyes were a little inflamed in their pouches.

"Good time!" said Doc and he went back to the laboratory with his cold beer. He made a peanut butter sandwich to eat with his beer. It was very quiet in the street. No one went by at all. Doc heard music in his head—violas and cellos, he thought. And they played cool, soft, soothing music with nothing much to distinguish it. He ate his sandwich and sipped his beer and listened to the music. When he had finished his beer, Doc went into the kitchen, and cleared the dirty dishes out of the sink. He ran hot water in it and poured soap chips under the running water so that the foam stood high and white. Then he moved about collecting all the glasses that weren't broken. He put them in the soapy hot water. The steak plates were piled high on the stove with their brown juice and their white grease sticking them together. Doc cleared a place on the table for the clean glasses as he washed them. Then he unlocked the

door of the back room and brought out one of his albums
of Gregorian music and he put a Pater Noster and Ag-
nus Dei on the turntable and started it going. The an-
gelic, disembodied voices filled the laboratory. They
were incredibly pure and sweet. Doc worked carefully
washing the glasses so that they would not clash together and spoil the music. The boys' voices carried the
melody up and down, simply but with the richness that
is in no other singing. When the record had finished,
Doc wiped his hands and turned it off. He saw a book
lying half under his bed and picked it up and he sat
down on the bed. For a moment he read to himself but
then his lips began to move and in a moment he read
aloud—slowly, pausing at the end of each line.

Even now
I mind the coming and talking of wise men from
    towers
Where they had thought away their youth. And I,
    listening,
Found not the salt of the whispers of my girl,
Murmur of confused colors, as we lay near sleep;
Little wise words and little witty words,
Wanton as water, honied with eagerness.

In the sink the high white foam cooled and ticked as
the bubbles burst. Under the piers it was very high
tide and the waves splashed on rocks they had not
reached in a long time.

Even now
I mind that I loved cypress and roses, clear,
The great blue mountains and the small gray hills,

The sounding of the sea. Upon a day
I saw strange eyes and hands like butterflies;
For me at morning larks flew from the thyme
And children came to bathe in little streams.

Doc closed the book. He could hear the waves beat
under the piles and he could hear the scampering of
white rats against the wire. He went into the kitchen
and felt the cooling water in the sink. He ran hot water
into it. He spoke aloud to the sink and the white rats,
and to himself:

Even now,
I know that I have savored the hot taste of life
Lifting green cups and gold at the great feast.
Just for a small and a forgotten time
I have had full in my eyes from off my girl
The whitest pouring of eternal light—

He wiped his eyes with the back of his hand. And
the white rats scampered and scrambled in their
cages. And behind the glass the rattlesnakes lay still
and stared into space with their dusty frowning eyes.